AF486688

PREY FOR RABBIT

HOLIDAY HORRORS

AIDEN PIERCE

Copyright © 2024 by Aiden Pierce.
All rights reserved.
No portion of this book may be reproduced in any form without written permission from the publisher or author, except as permitted by U.S. copyright law.

Cover Designer: Books and Moods
Editor: Killing It Write
Formatter: Open Bookish Creations

 Created with Vellum

A WORD OF WARNING

Prey for Rabbit is a dark shifter romance containing graphic content that may be triggering for some.

Trigger/Content Warnings: Murder, gore, sibling/parental loss, light body horror, violence, choking, knife/ax play, dubious consent, primal play, biting, marking, fear play, ritualistic sacrifices, monster appendages, size difference, breeding without pregnancy, light pseudo-necrophilia (necro fantasy) and other graphic sexual content.

Your mental health matters.

ONE

RUTH

"Hope Doyle."

Hope shot to her feet when she heard her name called out, bouncing on her heels. "I've been chosen!"

I stared at the back of my cousin's head from where she sat in our meeting hall, several rows up. Even from this distance, I could feel her elation at being selected while the rest of the room clapped.

Goosebumps exploded over my skin as I swiveled my gaze around at the mass of rabbit shifters, unable to keep the bewildered expression off my face.

Brainwashed. Every last one of them.

Why else would they be so eager to throw Hope to the wolves?

I understood the need to uphold the truce. Only the blood of our kind calmed the twisted hunger that cursed the wolfpack in these parts. If we didn't provide sacrifices, they'd lose control of their beasts, and things would go back to the way they were centuries before the truce. We'd lose so much more than three of our own every spring.

Better to keep the carnage to one day a year.

Still, it didn't explain why everyone treated the grisly event like it was something to look forward to. As if it was an honor to be chosen. The whole thing was serious *Hunger Games* fuckery, only there was no chance of fighting your way out.

Getting your name drawn out of that hat was a brutal death sentence, and Hope was acting like she'd just won the damn lottery.

Her parents sat beside her, beaming with pride at their daughter's selection. Just like my parents had when my sister's name was drawn last year. A chill worked through me as I recalled how proud Mom and Dad had been. *Proud* to drop my sister off in the middle of the woods to be hunted down and torn apart by wolves.

I wondered if other bunny burrows around the country were as cult-like as ours.

"Can't you even pretend to be happy for your cousin?" My father leaned over from where he sat beside me, his whisper harsh in my ear. "Hope knows what an honor it is to uphold the tradition of the Hunt. Her sacrifice will ensure our colony can live in peace for the rest of the year."

The blood turned cold in my veins. That's exactly what he'd said when Sarah's name had been drawn last year.

I tried not to hate my family for being so thoroughly brainwashed by the Elders of our burrow. We were born into it, just like the twenty other families that called it home. We'd all grown up with the story of how the Hunt and the truce came to be.

Three hundred or so years ago, there'd been a war between the bunny shifters in our area and the wolf shifters. A war we nearly lost because, well, bunnies—even in crazy numbers—were no match for predators ten times our size. They nearly slaughtered the entire colony.

The beast that lives inside every werewolf is like its own separate entity—monsters that live inside men. And the best thing to keep them sated and in control of their shifting powers? Rabbit shifter blood.

So, a truce between their kind and ours was struck.

The following Easter—because who could resist that irony?—our colony provided three young sacrifices to be set loose in the woods that sat between our territories.

The Hunt was born, and since then, once a year, the soil of the woods is bathed in bunny blood, which satisfies the wolves and gives them better control over their bestial hunger for the rest of the year.

From birth, we're taught that the good of the colony comes first.

Work. Obey. Breed. Die. Repeat.

That is our duty.

Bunny shifters, especially our colony, don't take much stock in fated mates like the rest of the shifter world. Our kind doesn't usually create bonds. The Elders don't take much stock in meaningful connections. All that matters is that we create more drones.

Bunnies have a reputation for being fervent breeders, and our burrow is no exception. Maybe that's why no one batted an ear at losing a son or daughter to the Hunt. They had a dozen more to fill the hole.

My parents had thirteen children altogether. After Sarah died, they were down to twelve. Every time she came up in conversation, all they talked about was how proud they were of her. As if she'd gone off to college and she'd be back for Christmas. It was probably just their way of coping.

Me, I couldn't do that shit. My anger wouldn't allow me to sit back and pretend like all this wasn't totally fucked.

I hadn't always hated how things worked here, but that was before Sarah died.

"Sawyer Keys."

I froze at the next name called. Sawyer Keys. He's my age, twenty-four. I've known him all my life. He'd always picked on me in school. Years later, he'd asked me if I'd be his mate. I'd refused him. After shredding his paper-thin ego, he'd gotten off on making my life hell.

Now he was going to die.

I searched the crowded meeting hall for Sawyer. Our eyes locked.

There wasn't so much as a twinge of happiness on his face like my cousin exhibited. He had a better understanding of what was in store for him. After a moment of intense eye contact, Sawyer ripped his attention away from me and put it back on the Elder who'd pulled his name. A beat later, he gave a silent, dutiful nod.

It was all an act. Sawyer Keys didn't have so much as one brave bone in his body.

"That's a shame," my father grunted. "He would have been a good mate for you."

This wasn't the first time my parents suggested Sawyer as a mate. It was abnormal for a female bunny my age to have never taken a mate. Most of the girls my age had at least a few kits. I'd rather die a kitless spinster than be mated to someone like Sawyer.

I'd told my parents that plenty of times before, how I'd rather fuck a rotten carrot than carry Sawyer's offspring. This time, I kept my mouth shut. It didn't matter now. Tomorrow, he'd be dead, and all the bitter memories I shared with him would be just that. Memories.

"Ruth Thatch."

Every single eye in the room turned on me as the Elder called my name.

"Way to go, Ruthie!" Someone from the row behind me patted my back as if to congratulate me on a job well done.

As if I'd somehow *earned* this.

I was in the age group of eligible sacrifices, but I'd never really stressed about being selected. I guess there was a part of me that didn't care what happened to me... Not after Sarah had been selected last year.

Maybe a piece of me had already died with Sarah.

My father and mother turned toward me and gave me that same look they gave my sister when her name was called. Suddenly, the numbness was gone, and all I felt was pure, dark, dangerous *rage*.

CHAPTER

TWO

CARVER

Easter meant only one thing for my pack.

The Hunt.

It marked the one time of year when we were sanctioned to brutally hunt down and murder a few young rabbit shifters from the local bunny burrow. All for the sake of satiating the thing that made us what we were: werewolves.

It didn't work like it did in human books and movies. We didn't transform under the full moon. We could shift year-round at will so long as we maintained control of the wolf within. It took bunny shifter blood to calm that gnawing Hunger, and it would stay in our bloodstream for about a year...

I was different from my pack mates. I didn't need bunny blood to calm the wolf inside me. It had always been quiet and easy to control. I didn't need to murder to tame it.

Why was I like this? That was a question I'd asked myself ever since my first shift when all I felt was emptiness. It was twisted to admit, but I sometimes caught myself wishing for that same brutal bloodlust as my pack

6

members. It had to be better than feeling nothing at all from the thing inside me that was supposed to be my entire identity.

Even my twin brother had the Hunger.

"You sure you don't want to join the Hunt?" my brother asked, frowning as he watched me load the cooler of beer into the back of my old Toyota truck.

"Not this shit again, Case." Irritation underscored my every syllable. "You ask me every year, and my answer is always the same. Do I have to get it stamped on my fucking forehead to have you get the damn picture?"

Casey scrubbed the back of his head with his hand and gave a shrug. "I guess I'm just hoping you'll say yes this time. I want to hunt with my brother."

"We go hunting together all the time."

"Yeah. With guns," my twin scoffed. "Not as fun as carnivore style, in full shift."

"You know shifting's not the same for me."

I slammed the tailgate shut, and Case pushed closer, lounging his arm on the back of my truck while dropping his voice. "You know there's nothing like running through the woods Easter day. This would be the perfect time to bond with the pack. Try to fit in."

I shot the silver-haired wolf a hot glare as I shoved my hand in my shirt pocket and fished out the squished pack of cigarettes, plucking one out and lighting it. "How many times do I have to tell you that I don't give a single fuck about blending in?"

There was conviction in my words, but they hadn't always been true. There'd been a time, not so long ago, that I cared about fitting in with the only family I'd ever known.

"Look." Casey sighed, waving away the cloud of cigarette smoke spiraling between us. "Lars has been talking shit again. I just think joining the Hunt will get him off your ass."

My muscles tensed at the mention of our alpha. "Lars has been talking shit since we were kids. That son of a bitch loves to run his jaw, nothing new."

My twin's brows gnashed as he helped himself to a cigarette and a light. "Come on, Carver. Now that he's alpha, the pack actually listens to the shit he spews. He's been telling them your beast doesn't speak to you, says that it's rejected you."

"Asshole has to get a damn hobby if all he has to talk about is me," I mumbled. "Anyway, it's true, isn't it? I can shift just like everyone else."

"Yeah, but..." He swept his eyes over the driveway of the packhouse where some of the others gathered, preparing to head into the woods for the Hunt. The promise of prey blood come sundown had the air hot and buzzing with bloodlust. Confident that no one was listening, Casey turned back to me with a weighted expression etched on his face. "Your beast doesn't speak to you."

It wasn't a question. He knew. He was the only one I'd ever told.

"So?"

He chewed on the butt of the cigarette dangling from his lips. "What's it like? Not having a mental link with it?"

I didn't like talking about it, and he knew that. Normally, he didn't press the subject.

"It's quiet," I answered with a low growl, warning him I wasn't in the mood to discuss this now. The sun was setting, and I needed to prepare for my role in the Hunt. I wouldn't be an active participant, but I had a job to do just like everyone else.

"It's gotta be weird not having a voice in your head

constantly telling you to murder and maim. Even if you don't need to sate the Hunger, joining the Hunt might make the rumors go away."

"I ate part of your kill last year. Doesn't that count as participation?"

It had been a year ago to the day, and I could still taste that poor girl on my tongue. Her fear had made her flesh sour and sweet all at once. It had taken everything in me to stomach the few bites I'd taken.

I'd decided that would be the last I ever try to "fit in" with my pack. And it hadn't been worth it anyway since my wolf hadn't so much as a twitch of a reaction.

Casey grinned at the mention of the sacrifice he'd killed last Hunt. "Sorry. Doesn't count. Eating a sacrifice and being the wolf to catch it are two different things. The wolves who catch the sacrifices are always worshiped for the rest of the year. Good way to get a mate. It's how I pulled Lila."

Like magic, the small woman with wavy black hair appeared seemingly out of nowhere and wrapped her arms around my brother's waist. "What are we talking about?"

Case twisted around to pull Lila into his arms and kissed the top of her head. "How being one of the wolves to kill a sacrifice in the Hunt is the best way to win a beautiful mate."

"You think you won me because of your trophy kill?" Lila playfully patted her mate's face, knocking the cigarette from his mouth. "That's so cute. Everyone knows my wolf chose yours because of looks, babe. And since you and Carver are identical twins, she just eenie-meenie-moed that shit."

Casey nipped playfully at Lila's ear, growling that low growl that had her turning to putty in his arms. His hands slid to her belly, which was just starting to show with their unborn cub.

I abruptly turned on my heel and opened the door to my truck. Before I could climb in, Case was in my way.

"Hey, think about what I said, yeah? Taking a mate might help you fit in better. Might get Lars off your ass. And you can't just wait around for your wolf to select a true mate for you. Since it doesn't speak to you, it might never—"

I grabbed my brother by the collar of his shirt and slammed him against the side of my truck. Everyone turned to look at us, but I didn't care. "I'm going to say this one last time. I don't need a mate. So just give it a rest," I snarled louder than I meant to.

"Yeah, give it a rest, Casey. Don't you know your brother is content living alone in his cabin, rutting his right hand forever? Probably for the best he doesn't mate. Wouldn't want to risk spreading whatever's wrong with his wolf to a cub."

I released my brother and slowly turned to find Lars standing behind me.

Our alpha was shorter and had a slighter build than me. I could take him in a fight, in either form. I wanted nothing more than to sucker punch him in the gut. Too bad initiating any physical contact with the pack leader was regarded as an official challenge for the place as alpha. That meant a fight to the death.

It would be fun being the reason this asshole breathed his last breath, but I had no interest in leading the pack. So, I settled with flipping him off, accompanied by a terse grin that was all teeth, before climbing into my truck.

"Carver, come on. I was just trying—"

My brother's protest was cut short as I slammed my

door shut, jammed the key into the ignition and tore out of the driveway in a spray of gravel.

The truth was, it wasn't Casey who I was pissed at. It was the beast inside me.

The curse didn't seem to affect me in the same way it did my pack, and somehow, that made me more broken than the rest.

My role during the Hunt was simple: plant the sacrifices in the woods—spread them out so there was more sport in it for the pack—and keep humans away the rest of the night.

I sat in a lawn chair in my truck bed, my beer cooler open at my feet with a cold can in my hand and my hunting rifle slung across my thighs. I'd parked along the backroad that ran alongside the woods, beside the bullet-riddled sign that read "PRIVATE PROPERTY – Trespassers Will Be Shot!"

A little nothing town with a population somewhere in the triple digits was nearby. Centuries have passed since our kind messed with the humans before our truce with the bunnies. The stories faded from their memories, and now they just peg the bunny shifters as hippies and us wolves as crazy backwoods hicks. They've stayed away from our territory for the most part.

As dusk started to settle, headlights appeared down the road some ways. I took a sip from my beer, eyes narrowing on the station wagon that pulled up beside my truck. Downing the last of my beer, I tossed the can to my feet, slung my gun over my shoulder and jumped to the ground.

I slowly approached the vehicle. A magnetic sign was slapped to the station wagon's faux wooden siding reading "Watership Farms. Fresh produce since 1792."

The driver was the same guy who'd been delivering to us since I'd taken on this role for the pack. He was a smug son of a bitch who thought he was safe from us. One day, we'd probably kill him too, sacrifice or not.

He rolled down his window, giving me a flimsy smile while shoving his fingers through his greasy, thinning hair. I didn't miss the way his hand shook.

"Aw, nervous, Doug?" I wasn't sure if I remembered his name correctly, and I didn't care. "For how long we've been doing this, you'd think we'd be old friends by now." I folded my arms on the car door and leaned into the open window. This rabbit shifter was shaking like a damn leaf in a windstorm. He didn't know my wolf might as well be vegan for its complete lack of interest in rabbit blood. Still, instincts told me this male was a grade above scum, so I took pleasure in rattling him.

"G—got you a fresh batch."

I nodded. "Good. Love your deliveries. Always fresh. Should really try your produce sometime."

Missing the sarcasm in my tone, Doug went along with it, laughing. "Y—yeah. Carrots got that same kind of crunch as bunny bones, I bet."

My expression morphed into something savage, and Doug's nervous smile evaporated in an instant. "I'm sorry—"

"Hey, I'm the big bad wolf here. I'm going to make unsavory jokes about my pack's dinner. We do love playing with our food, after all. But jokes like that about your own kind, some of them probably blood too—knowing you lot and how you love to shag your cousins—that's just sick, Doug." I laughed and hated how empty it sounded.

The truth was, I hated this entire ritual, hated marching the bunnies to their deaths. But this was the way of the pack. I didn't care about pack laws and traditions. Casey did. And my twin brother was just about the only person or thing on this planet that made me feel something.

Ignoring the driver's pathetic apologies, I peered into the back seat, where three young rabbit shifters sat shoulder to shoulder.

One—a blonde-haired girl in a sundress of all things, almost looked eager. Last year's bunch had all been pretty bright-eyed and bushy-tailed, just like her. Poor bastards. Their burrow really had them brainwashed. They were just as eager to die as my pack was to kill them.

Next to her sat a male with unkempt brown hair and dark, beady eyes that had me on edge for reasons I couldn't peg. That one seemed more in touch with reality by his somber expression.

The second girl with wild, hateful eyes struck me the most. Her jet-black hair was tied up in a haphazard bun on top of her head, with a streak of purple dye running through it. Her ears were full of silver rings, and a septum piercing decorated her button nose.

I wondered if the purple stripe translated to her shifted form, and I couldn't help but imagine a black bunny with ears full of hoops and a shock of purple across its black pelt.

Her chocolate brown eyes locked with mine, and the pure loathing behind them stabbed me in the gut like an ice-cold knife.

For the first time ever, the beast inside me stirred—hungry for a taste of bunny blood.

THREE

RUTH

The back road running through the woods was nothing but dirt, making for a bumpy ride that did nothing to ease the budding dread in my gut.

I'd never been this nervous in my life. It wasn't every day someone was casually driven to their own brutal blood sacrifice.

To make matters worse, Doug was responsible for delivering the sacrifices this year.

Doug was the High Elder's oldest son, and he was a fucking tool.

There was no convincing him to turn back and let us go. I would swear he got enjoyment out of sending young rabbit shifters to their deaths.

All my hatred for Doug found a new target when we pulled off on the side of the road behind a beat-up truck that looked older than me, and a man approached.

The headlights from our car lit him up like a spotlight. *He had a gun*—a hunting rifle.

His eyes glinted in the light like some monster in the night. He wore a worn black shirt with a faded logo I couldn't make out and dark denim jeans that hugged his brawny frame, touting the power packed in his lean muscle.

You were supposed to be able to tell the color of their wolf's fur by the color of their human hair. This man's hair was silver. His pale hair was a shock against the dark swath of tattoos covering his body—his forearms, his throat. A barbed wire design even stretched from the edge of his sharp jaw and followed the perimeter of his hairline.

This guy's whole vibe was backwoods cutthroat. He had no right to be so damn attractive. For all I knew, this was one of the wolves who'd eaten my sister.

He prowled toward my window, peering into the back seat.

Some of Hope's excitement seemed to thin as she took in the approaching werewolf. "Is that one of the wolves? Why does he have a gun? Doesn't he know we're the sacred sacrifices?"

I turned on her, blinking. "What were you expecting? A red carpet? Wake the hell up, Hope. We're about to be hunted down and eaten by wolves."

Her lower lip trembled, and her sky-blue eyes filled with tears. "Don't you think I know that? But we're doing our duty to keep our burrow safe. Our sacrifice is going to save lives. I'm proud of that. I just thought…"

"That they'd be more appreciative of what we're doing for them," Sawyer muttered.

The tightness in my chest made each breath I took short and shallow as I watched the man approach the driver's side window.

"Predators don't respect their food," I murmured.

The werewolf kept his gaze on me the entire time he spoke with Doug. Even as he pointed to Hope. "You first."

My cousin glanced at me, and the look in her eyes drove a knife into my heart.

I'd always thought my cousin to be kind of an idiot who just did what she was told. But in these last moments I knew I had with her, I saw her in a different light. She was just making the best out of a situation she had no control over. She'd been told by our Elders and her own parents that this was her *duty* to the colony.

So, Hope, being the good girl that she was, was going to do this with a smile on her face.

Even if she was screaming on the inside.

Me? I had no intention of being so compliant.

Hope moved to get out of the car, but I reached across Sawyer and snatched her wrist, preventing her from leaving. "Let's go together."

The male's jaw flexed, and something almost akin to amusement flickered over his inked face. "Yeah, see, that's not how this works, Little Bunny. Say your goodbyes now."

"It's okay..." At Hope's brave smile, an uncomfortable pang burrowed into my gut. Nothing about this situation was anything close to okay.

I wanted to comfort her, to tell her to run as hard as she could. But there was no time. She pulled her wrist from my grip, opened her door and disappeared into the woods with the gunman.

Sawyer stared into the darkness that enveloped Hope. Without turning to face me, his hand crept over to mine and gripped it tightly. I resisted the urge to shake him off. At that moment, we needed each other.

Doug flipped on the radio and leaned back in his chair, humming along to John Denver's "Country Roads."

My mind grappled with what to do. My list of options was slim. We weren't given any time to prepare, but one of my brothers had managed to press a small pocket knife into my hands while hasty goodbyes were given.

Doug wasn't armed. He had no reason to be. Every Sacrifice was so thoroughly brainwashed that every bunny before me happily flocked to their slaughter.

Except me.

I'd just started to imagine sinking the blade into the back of his fat neck when the silver-haired male reappeared. Doug started to get out, but the werewolf was already at the door, ripping it open.

He gestured for Sawyer to get out of the car. "You next."

The man's eyes flicked to my hand clasped in Sawyer's. Something almost akin to pity flickered behind his eyes, but it was gone in a blink.

"Kiss your mate goodbye." A chill skipped up my spin at the werewolf's expression. "If you're quick, I'll even let you have one last rut."

Before I could inform the man that we weren't mates, Sawyer was on top of me.

Panic clawed its way up my throat as a horrible sense of déjà vu set in. Sawyer pushed me onto my back and crammed his tongue into my mouth. His hand greedily palmed my breast, giving it a rough squeeze that had me gasping in pain and shock.

In my periphery, Doug twisted around in his seat to get a good look at us. He knew Sawyer and I weren't mates, but the creep was more than happy to watch the assault.

I resisted the urge to bury my knife in his fucking eye socket—not wanting to reveal I was armed—and instead settled for a punch to Sawyer's nose. There was a sickening crunch followed by a spray of blood. It peppered my face, leaving the taste of his tongue in my mouth and his scent in my nose.

My stomach heaved.

"Crazy bitch!" Sawyer shrieked, reeling back to nurse his nose with both hands. "You're really gonna turn down an opportunity to live for a few minutes longer?"

I glared up at Sawyer. "I'd rather be torn apart by wolves than mate with you."

Sawyer raised his fist, ready to hit me back, but he froze with a look of terror in his eyes.

The gunman had the barrel of his hunting rifle pressed against the back of the rabbit shifter's skull. "You heard her."

Sawyer's breath came out in a rattle. He slowly climbed out of the car, and I watched as the wolf took Sawyer off into the darkness to disappear from my life forever.

I wiped the blood from my face with an angry swipe of my hand, watching it smear in the rear-view mirror as I glared at our driver's reflection. "You piece of steaming shit. You were just gonna sit there and let him do whatever he wanted, weren't you?"

Doug licked his lips as he eyed me in the rearview mirror. "Too prude to do what bunnies do best, huh? Can't spread your legs even if it means living longer."

My fingers tightened around the knife in my pocket as I fantasized gutting him, taking his keys and shoving his body into the road. Maybe running him over before driving as far as the tank of gas would get me.

Movement outside the window drew my attention from Doug for a beat, long enough to see the silver-haired male had returned from the woods. Alone. Whatever he'd done with Hope and Sawyer, there was no sign of them now.

Still unwilling to reveal my knife, I released the handle and lunged for Doug's seat. Taking the seatbelt, I wrapped it around his throat and brought my body weight down to the floor behind him. He coughed and sputtered, desperately pulling at the strap before realizing there wasn't any hope of overpowering me. He fumbled with the door handle, shifted into a sable rabbit and bolted out the open door.

On my next breath, my door wrenched open, and I was pulled out of the station wagon.

"Oh, we have a feisty one on our hands this year. You're going to be the reason Watership Farms gets prison-grade security vans."

I glared up at the silver-haired male while trying to wrench my arm from his hold. It was useless. Even in his human form, he towered over me. He had to be freaking gigantic in his true shape. And he was *hot*, literally and figuratively. His body heat bled into my clothes, filling me with fire.

My eyes dragged over his broad chest, up his tatted throat, to meet his eyes. They were gray, like angry storm clouds.

I'd spotted some of the wolf shifters on my rare trips to the nearby town to buy supplies the burrow couldn't produce. It had always been at a distance. Up close, I could sense the beast hiding beneath his skin.

He was as gorgeous as he was terrifying. And now Doug was gone—or hiding, the coward—leaving me alone with the silver-haired monster.

FOUR

CARVER

For the first time ever, I hungered for bunny blood. No. I hungered for *her*.

The black and purple-haired bunny shifter radiated violence and fury so palpable I could taste it. She'd nearly strangled the driver with his own seatbelt, and before that, she'd sucker-punched that other male bunny in the nose and broken it, judging by how much blood he'd spewed.

The sight of her pale cheeks speckled with the blood of that male had my mouth watering and my cock rock hard.

I was wrong about her being mated to him... So why did she carry traces of his scent? Maybe they had history. Whatever it was, I should have ripped out his throat for the way this girl looked at him. He'd clearly hurt her.

Fuck. Why did I care? I didn't know shit about these people. They were here for one purpose: To feed my pack.

"Follow me." I pushed forward into the woods, leaves crunching as her tiny legs worked to keep up with my stride.

"Shouldn't I go first? What if I shift and run?"

Without turning around, I patted the rifle slung on my shoulder. "Easy. I'll just shoot you. I'm an excellent shot, even with small game."

"I'm a fast runner."

"Can't outrun a bullet."

I kept walking as I waited for the sound of her shift, something resembling anxiety pulling low in my gut.

I'd hate to shoot her. Her death was inevitable, but something about her presence roused my wolf. It felt closer to the surface than usual, and I wanted to savor it. So, the longer I could prolong my time with this curious bunny, the better.

The tension in my stomach loosened when she seemed to decide against chancing an escape and jogged to keep up with me.

"Why does a werewolf need a gun anyway? Why not shift and hunt me down? Isn't that why I'm here?"

"The Hunt doesn't start until midnight." I didn't bother telling her I didn't like to shift. I didn't like giving over control to something I didn't consider an ally.

"Where did you take Hope and Sawyer?"

"Planted them in different parts of the woods. It makes it more of a challenge to find all three of you, and it limits the chances of one wolf killing more than one sacrifice. Makes it fair."

"Fair?" Her voice jumped an octave, frightening a bird from a nearby thicket. "It's hilarious to pretend even for a second that werewolves understand the concept of fairness."

Stopping in my tracks, I whipped around to face her, and she nearly crashed into my chest.

"Listen carefully. You have a small—a *very* small chance of making it out of these woods before one of my kind catches you. But it's still a chance. Your odds of surviving drop to zero if you annoy me to the point where I snap your neck before the Hunt can even start. *Capiche*, Little Bunny?"

Her eyes sparked with defiance. "I'm not afraid of you."

She was lying. Her heart thrashed so hard in her chest that I practically felt it on the tip of my tongue. "All bunnies are afraid of wolves. It's instinct for you."

"My hate is stronger than any instinct."

I wasn't sure what response I expected, but it wasn't that. All I could do was stare at her for a tense beat.

I'd been doing this job, escorting rabbit shifters to their death, for years. No sacrifice was ever like her—spiteful and full of fire. She was far too alive for someone doomed to die.

There was something magnetic about this little female that had me bending to breathe her in. The sweet aroma of her lavender shampoo and something else that was uniquely her filtered into my lungs. Her scent was like smelling salts, rousing something inside me to life.

My wolf. This was the closest I'd ever felt to it. Being close to this bunny shifter seemed to rouse it.

A sinister idea unfurled in my mind. Maybe I could make it speak to me.

I wasn't particularly drawn to the idea of scaring her, but I'd do anything to connect with the beast inside me.

She must have sensed the danger boiling just below the surface of my skin as she started to back away from me, her eyes flaring wide. "What's wrong with you?"

I took a step toward her, then another. She slowly backed away—her instincts telling her to keep as much distance between us as possible. Her back hit a tree. Christ, she was small. She had to crane her head to glare up at me.

For a beat, she looked as though she was about to make

a break for it. My threat to shoot her must have come back to her because she stayed rooted where she was.

I held out my hand. "Give me your clothes."

A barbed silence stretched between us. Not even the woods dared make a noise. The only sound was her hammering pulse.

"W—what?"

"You heard me." My lips curled into a cruel smirk. "Strip."

A delicious blush seared her cheeks, and a sweet feminine aroma bled from her thighs.

The wolf inside me growled, the sound coming out strangled and not my own.

Her scent intensified, making my hunger spike. My cock thickened in my jeans as I watched her squirm.

The venom in her look could kill a man. "I don't know what twisted game you're trying to play, but you can go fuck yourself."

"I'm not going to touch you," I assured her, though I wasn't sure I could keep my promise. Unlike the rest of my pack, my wolf was barely present, so I didn't need bunny blood to control it. But now it was hungry, ready to burst to the surface any moment. It never ripped control from my hands before. Maybe that was because it never had a reason to... Until now.

This girl had me second-guessing everything I thought I knew about the monster inside me.

"Why do you want my clothes?"

"Protocol for the sacrifices," I lied.

She blinked. "What do you mean?"

"You'll freeze in your naked human form, and it will force you to shift. You're faster in your wild shape, giving us wolves more of a challenge. Plus, we won't have to cut you out of your clothes to eat you."

An involuntary gasp left her lips. "That's evil."

I gave a dark chuckle. "No, Little Bunny. That's nature. Wolves have eaten bunnies for as long as they've been around."

I held up a finger, enjoying how her eyes shot wide as my nail extended into a vicious claw. I hooked it into the zipper of her jacket and slowly tugged it open.

She moved so fast I could barely track her hand as it shoved into her pocket and brandished a knife. The blade flashed as she slammed it toward my heart. I caught her wrist just as the tip punctured my flesh.

There was a prick of pain—but the pleasure that followed drowned out the discomfort. My wolf liked watching this bold female try to go toe-to-toe with me. Everything about her seemed to lure my wolf closer to the surface. This discovery encouraged me to double down on my plan to tease and torment her.

The girl winced as my fingers tightened around her wrist, and I jerked on her arm to pluck the blade from my chest, grinning at the sight of my blood streaking down the blade.

"Looks like our little bunny has claws."

Lars wouldn't like it if he knew I was toying with one of the sacrifices before the Hunt. But I didn't give a shit. She was the best shot at getting my wolf to speak to me.

"What's your name, Stabby Little Rabbit?"

She swallowed hard. "Ruth... It's Ruth."

I grinned. "Is that short for ruthless?"

Her eyes narrowed into slits. "Do wolves always play with their food?"

"Not always. But my meals are never as interesting as

you." I released my hold on her wrist while wrenching the knife from her fingers. I pointed the blade at her, the knife's point scraping the hollow of her throat.

My cock ached at the way some of my blood smeared her flesh. She looked so pretty covered in me.

"Let's make this interesting," I hummed. "You're going to run... And I'm going to catch you. Neither of us will shift. We'll save that for the Hunt. If I catch you, I'll cut you out of your clothes myself. Deal?"

Ruth said nothing. Instead, she took off running.

I couldn't keep the smirk off my face as I watched her bolt into the dark, hanging back a moment to give her a head start.

"I'll take that as a yes."

CHAPTER

FIVE

RUTH

Instinct took over the moment the wolf told me to run. I'd cover more ground in a shorter time if I shifted. He told me not to, but what were the chances he'd be able to shoot me in time? A vicious shiver tore through me, colder than the wind that whipped my hair. I had a feeling he wasn't bluffing about being an excellent shot. Even if he was, it was a wonder his wolf hadn't taken over yet.

If I morphed into my rabbit form, I doubt the monster inside him would resist. It didn't give a damn if the Hunt hadn't officially started. Instinct didn't give a shit about rules.

But it wasn't the fear of the bullet or being hunted by a fully shifted werewolf that kept me in my human form. It was the dark thrill of imagining him cutting my clothes off with my own knife.

Jesus. What in the ever-loving fuck was wrong with me? Why was I so attracted to this monster?

For all I knew, he was the alpha of the pack, and he was toying with me for shits and giggles until the Hunt officially started. If he was the one to kill me, wearing that cocky

26

smirk while he sunk his teeth into me, shredding my clothes with his rough hands... There had to be worse ways to go.

A small, inexplicable part of me *wanted* him to catch me. And it was that epiphany that frightened me more than anything else. These woods—this male—they were screwing with my head.

Even on two legs, I zipped through the trees. Outrunning predators was second nature.

Snapping twigs and crunching leaves from behind got louder as he gained on me. I didn't have to look back to know the precious space between us was shrinking fast. My breath came out in harsh gusts, my heart pounded hard in my head like an alarm.

You're going to run, and I'm going to catch you.

The ghost of his words haunted me. Not because they struck fear into my heart, but because they filled me with a fire that I was all too familiar with...

My heat cycle was near. A female bunny's heat was always intense and impossible to control. There was no stopping it. Why *now?* And why was it this creepy werewolf and his psychotic games shaking my hormones awake? It explained that little part of me that wanted to be caught. Stupid bunny libido. Didn't it know this male only saw me as dinner?

Adrenaline slammed through my system. My legs pumped harder as I shot through the dark, and as my speed picked up, so did the male's.

A sick sensation roiled in my gut, one that told me this chase could be over as quickly as it started. The wolf was playing with me. He wanted his own hunt before he had to share me with the rest of his pack.

What was I doing? It didn't matter how horny I was.

This wasn't a game. The werewolf didn't want to mate with me. He wanted to slaughter and eat me.

I started to shift, but a muscular body slammed into me, and a large hand wrapped around the base of my rabbit ears. My knife's point found my throat.

"Finish shifting, and I'll gut you right here, Ruthless," the wolf snarled, his face shoving into mine.

My head spun. I was stuck in half form—still human, save for the big floppy bunny ears and fluffy tail pushing against the back of my jeans.

I winced as the man's grip tightened around my ears, and he slowly walked me backward until my back hit a tree. His steely eyes combed over my ears, and something almost akin to a genuine smile lurked at the corner of his mouth. He brought the knife up from my throat and hooked the tip of the blade through one of the hoops adorning my ears.

"Your bunny ears are pierced."

"They don't just disappear when I shift, asshole. And I hate to break it to you..." I forced a saccharine smile. "But that's not the only place I have piercings. Your meal is gonna be full of metal."

The male's eyes flashed. Something dark and dangerous lurked behind those storm-gray orbs.

"One, two, three..." He tapped my piercings one by one with the end of the knife, creating a little metal jolt each time. "Four, five, six."

He slipped the knife down my shirt and, with a swift motion, started to cut my clothes off. A scream flew past my lips. His hand released my ears and slammed over my mouth.

"*Quiet.* The Hunt hasn't started, but my pack might be near. Don't tempt them with your screams. I'm not in the mood to share."

I shivered, another flood of heat sweeping through my core.

His nostrils twitched. My breath froze in my lungs as he bent over me, buried his nose in my neck, and inhaled. "Fuuuuck," he rasped against me. "Why do you smell so damn good?"

This wolf could scent my pre-heat pheromones. I had to get out of here. If he had this kind of reaction to the scent all bunny shifter females gave off just before their cycle, what would he do when I went into full heat?

I winced against his palm as he kept cutting my upper layers off, the knife nicking my flesh as his ministrations grew hurried.

He said he wouldn't touch me.

I wanted to believe that, yet I couldn't shake the feeling that he was lying.

A few of the most intense seconds of my life crawled by on hands and knees as this strange man sliced through my shirt. Dropping his hand from my mouth, he tugged off the ruined fabric and tossed it away.

He leaned back, sucking in a breath as he took in my naked breasts. I didn't bother covering up. As shifters, we didn't have the same kind of embarrassment as humans when we were in the mood. When we shifted into our animal forms, our clothes would fall away, and when we turned back, we'd be naked.

The male drifted closer. His brutal heat swept over me like a caress, and his scent clotted in my lungs like a chloroform-soaked rag, making my head swim.

I bared my teeth when he took the knife and flicked the metal loop adorning one nipple, then the other, as he continued counting my piercings.

"Eight, nine..." He trailed it down my torso, applying

just enough pressure to leave an angry welt. Then he tapped the blade to my belly ring. "Ten."

With a flick of his wrist, he popped the button of my pants off. Slotting the flat of the blade between my jeans and my panties, he pulled back to pin me with a heated look. "Should I keep going? I have a feeling there's more."

My skin heated beneath the chill of the blade against my apex. Our eyes locked.

Something shifted behind his gaze. His muscles visibly tightened, his shoulders stiffening. His aura shifted, turning primal and violent. One minute, he'd been wickedly playful. Now, he was dominance incarnate.

His control over his wolf was slipping.

This female was trouble. She invaded my system like a fucking drug. I wanted to keep her safe from my pack only so I could devour her myself.

"We're not going to eat her. We're going to fuck her. Mate her. Breed her."

Every cell in my body froze. That voice. I'd never heard it before, but I knew who it belonged to. It had lived inside me all my life.

For the first time, my wolf finally spoke to me. Just my luck. It was telling me to do something that would get me exiled from my pack.

Fucking hell.

"No," I responded out loud. "Keeping her isn't an option."

Ruth blinked like she was trying to make sense of what I was saying. To her, it would appear that I was talking to myself. Realization seemed to creep in as if she was recalling that werewolves weren't like rabbit shifters. We had inner beasts that demanded we feed and fuck and breed—an instinct more monster than animal.

"Mate her."

No, this couldn't be happening. This had to be some sick joke my subconscious was making. My wolf was supposed to be my greatest strength, my identity. How could I live with this voice while it was telling me to commit something as unforgivable as mating a rabbit shifter? It wasn't done.

I shook my head. "Wolves don't make mating bonds with rabbits."

Ruth's breath audibly caught in her throat. That alluring scent flooded my nostrils, stronger than before.

Her kind had two major instincts.

Breed—Just like werewolves.

And survive. Run. Seek shelter. *Live.*

Which one she went with in this particular situation should have been a no-brainer. But something about me seemed to appeal to that first instinct, which only made my wolf more ravenous.

I tapped the blade against her pussy, grinning darkly. "You better run, Little Bunny before I do something to you we'll both regret."

"No! Don't let her go!"

I gritted my teeth and clenched my muscles until my nerves were screaming in pain, using every iota of strength to keep my wolf caged inside.

She could see I was struggling with my control, yet she stood there—frozen. A curious cocktail of terror, arousal and anger bled into the air, thick enough to chew. "I—"

"Fucking go before my beast breaks free and tears your pussy apart!"

This time, she jerked into action.

Dark fur sprang over her milky skin, her body shrinking and hitting the ground with a thud where her jeans were piled on the ground. A breath later, a black bunny with a purple streak of dye along its body leaped from underneath her clothes heaped on the ground and bounded away into the dark.

I stared after her for a beat before turning my attention to the knife in my hand, where her panties still dangled from the blade.

SEVEN

RUTH

I shot forward as my rabbit legs dug into the dirt like a spring with every step. My little heart thrummed as my mind spun out of whack, trying to process what in the flaming hell just happened.

Was that male's wolf telling him to claim me? That would mean... No. It couldn't be.

Predator shifters had a voice in their head that told them when to eat, when to sleep, when to do anything that catered to their animalistic nature. Sometimes, they'd choose a mate to bond and claim. The phenomenon was known as "fated mates" since some believed a coupling chosen by the beast was some kind of divine intervention.

That shit didn't happen between prey and predator shifters, especially not with a wolf and a rabbit. It wasn't natural. It probably wasn't even possible. A werewolf had to be shifted to give its mark.

He'd towered over me in human form, so I could only imagine how obscenely huge he would be as a fully shifted werewolf.

The size difference was... Impossible.

He'd break me.

A shiver shot down my tiny spine, making my fur stand straight. I didn't dare look back to see if his wolf had taken over to do what werewolves did best: *chase their prey*.

In my rabbit form, I could see in the dark, and we hadn't come all that far, so finding the road should have been easy. But there was something about these woods that twisted my senses and threw my natural sense of direction out of whack.

This land had been owned by the pack for hundreds of years. The trees were tall and ancient. Even the soil felt different, packed with magic and decades' worth of bunny blood from past sacrifices. It was as if the very trees were against me, doing everything to prevent my escape.

Maybe I'd run into Hope, and we could find a way out together. Sawyer could go fuck himself. I almost hoped he'd get caught and eaten by the wolves. That asshole deserved to be torn apart.

A terrifying howl split the night. Then another, and another. A dozen or so wolves howled, marking the start of the Hunt.

My adrenaline spiked with every passing second that I raced through the dark with no sign of the road or my cousin. I couldn't scent the wolves, but knew they weren't far. There was a strange kind of dark and ominous energy in the air, making it buzz.

Then, a scream echoed through the woods. My heart stopped. This wasn't the howl of a wolf. It was a woman's. *Hope!*

I bolted toward the scream, praying that I reached her before the wolves.

As soon as I saw them, I scrambled back into the safety of the underbrush before I could be seen.

Lying in a fetal position on the ground was a completely naked Hope. She was covered in scrapes and cuts, shivering, but not from the cold.

Five wolves surrounded her, although to call them wolves was a stretch.

This was the first time I'd ever seen a shifted werewolf. They were humanoid, hulking creatures covered in dense fur. Their heads were the most wolf-like feature, with thick human-like arms that ended with savage claws and large tooth-filled maws that snarled and snapped at their victim.

In that half-second, they pounced.

She managed another scream before a black wolf lunged at her, grabbing hold of her throat and ripping it open. Hope tore like she was made of tissue paper.

A spray of blood gushed from the gaping hole in her throat.

Another one of them bit into her stomach, wrapping their massive jaws completely around her body. It was followed by a sick, wet crunch.

It took a moment, but I managed the strength to look into her eyes.

She was still alive, and I think in her last moments, she saw me. She looked right at me but couldn't make a sound. It was a mercy when she went limp.

The wolves surrounded her, blocking off my view as they feasted on the dead girl.

Soaked in blood, they raised their heads and howled into the darkness above them. Some of them were so wet with it that it flattened their fur to their skulls and gave them the appearance of literal demons. Wasn't that what they were?

Fucking monsters.

At that moment, the clouds rolled back from the moon, and a shock of silver fur caught my attention. A silver wolf.

It was him.

Rage and grief and a miasma of a dozen other emotions paralyzed me for several harrowing seconds before instinct kicked in. *Run.*

I whipped around and dashed away, running until my lungs burned and the muscles in my little feet ached.

The pit in my stomach grew until it threatened to swallow me whole. I'd just watched my cousin get ripped apart by wolves, and it was more barbaric than I could have imagined. This was what happened to Sarah when she'd been chosen—surrounded by feral monsters who saw her as nothing but a meal, scared and alone, knowing her family had purposely sent her here.

It made me sick.

How could the Elders do this to us? How had they so thoroughly brainwashed our burrow into thinking this was the only means of keeping peace with the wolves?

I hated feeling so helpless, unable to do anything but run when faced with the injustice of this evil. But I was so tired of running.

It was as if something was listening to my thoughts, a deity that heard my prayers and decided to throw me a bone. A gleam of something bright and metallic through the trees caught my eye. I followed it into a clearing, and at its center was a stump. A ray of moonlight illuminated the object sticking from the stump like a spotlight.

It was an ax.

I shifted back to my human form and approached the stump. Grasping the worn handle, I tugged it free and held it up. The moonlight caught on the blade, making the sharp edge gleam like it was Excalibur, only I didn't feel like a knight in shining armor. I wasn't even wearing pants.

All I had was an old ax for a weapon and fury for armor.

CHAPTER

EIGHT

RUTH

I wandered through the dark, the ax clutched tight in my hand. Naked. Cold. *Pissed.* My anger burned my fear to ash. Now, I almost hoped they'd find me. I'd probably end up like Hope, but at least I'd shed some blood with my new steely friend.

Something shifted in the dark ahead of me, and I tightened my grip on the ax.

Glowing eyes emerged from the shadows. My grip tightened around the ax handle even more, my sweaty palms making it slick.

A werewolf prowled forward, its attention fastened on me. A guttural growl rumbled from its chest, making the hairs on my nape stand.

The black wolf that tore out Hope's throat. Her blood still dripped from its jowls.

It started to circle me, and I fought back against the instinct telling me to run. I couldn't take my ax with me if I shifted. And I was done being the prey.

As it stalked around me in a wide circle, I noticed the

swell of the monster's belly. A deep discomfort burrowed in my gut. This she-wolf was pregnant.

The female hunched, her yellow eyes honing on me as she prepared to pounce. I braced myself, ax at the ready.

Before the black wolf could pounce, another sprang forward from the dark. It was a huge wolf with a pale coat matted in blood.

A *silver* wolf.

It was him—The male who'd chased me through the woods, cut my shirt off, teased me with my knife...

And murdered my cousin while I watched from the bushes.

He placed himself between the black wolf and my ax, protecting her. Were they mates? I don't know why that angered me more. His vicious flirting hadn't been genuine. He'd just been playing with his food. That's all I was to him. A meal, just like the other sacrifices.

Not this time. Not with this rabbit.

"Don't fear, Little Rabbit. Your blood will make my pup strong," the beast rasped.

"I don't think so, motherfucker," I snarled back.

The silver werewolf laughed, the sound so deep and jarring it rattled me to the bone. "You're a bold one. The other sacrifices aren't so mouthy."

"We should give her to Carver," the black she-wolf mused from behind her mate. "He likes the sassy ones. Like the purple-haired girl from last year. Called her tasty."

The purple-haired girl from last year? A chill washed over me. Sarah had purple hair. The same color that I streaked my hair with—a silly little way I liked to remember her.

The wolf that killed Sarah was named Carver. If I lived through this night, I'd remember that name.

The silver wolf pounced. He was heavy, and with my angle and reflexes, his weight was his downfall. I didn't even have to swing. All I had to do was raise the ax at the right moment and hold it where his throat would land.

A shockwave of pain jolted down my arms at the impact. A warm flood of blood coated my arms. I rolled out from beneath him just in time to avoid being crushed. I placed my foot on his body, using it as leverage to wrench the ax free.

Blood spurted from the gash in his neck to the rhythm of his heartbeat. It was slowing down.

Pure anger drove me as I lifted the ax and brought it down hard on his thick neck, again and again, until I'd separated the beast's massive head from his body.

The dark-furred wolf shifted into a gorgeous, curvy woman with a thick mane of dark curly hair. She stumbled to her knees, taking the wolf's great head in her arms. "Casey! Oh god, no. Casey!"

If I lived through this night, the woman's horrified shriek would haunt me for the rest of my days.

Blood pooled underneath her dead mate, and I was amazed by how much was in him.

Clutching his severed head to her chest, she lifted her face, her tear-swollen cheeks glistening in the moonlight. Our eyes locked.

There was no anger in her expression, only despair. It was almost like she was pleading with me to kill her, too. My gaze drifted down to her naked, swollen belly. Something akin to humanity jerked me from my rage and I turned on my heel, bolting into the dark.

After an unknown stretch of time spent wandering the woods, I found the road again. I could almost cry from the relief. So long as I followed it, I'd find something. Ideally, the way out.

My heart fell when a cabin appeared ahead. It wasn't the main road leading back to town, but at least it was something.

This was still pack property, so I had to be careful.

Cautiously, I tip-toed up the porch and peered inside. The place was dark. There was no car parked out front. No fresh scent clung to the door. No one was home.

Normally, I wouldn't barge into a cabin that was, in all likelihood, owned by a werewolf, but desperation made me bold. Or stupid. I'd figure out which once I was inside.

I tried the front door and found it unlocked. I pushed inside and went rigid the moment the scent hit me. Tanned leather and pine, with the faintest hint of cigarette smoke.

I recognized that scent... I'd stumbled right into the home of the silver wolf.

It was almost too perfect. He was dead. He wasn't going to be coming home. But what about his mate?

I took in a deep breath, my brows pulling together in confusion. There was no trace of another's scent. The cabin was small, decorated sparsely, with no sign of a female's touch. Maybe his mate lived back at the main pack house?

Then again, I didn't detect his scent on her skin, so maybe they weren't even bonded mates.

But... the way she'd cried for him...

I shook my head and pushed the fresh memory to the back of my mind. Nope. That would be something to unpack in therapy later, assuming I'd survive this nightmare.

I kept the lights off as I wandered deeper into the cabin, not wanting to signal to the wolves that someone was home in case anyone happened by.

My eyes adjusted to the dark to take in the dead man's belongings.

"Ugh. Creepy," I muttered to myself as I found several sets of blank eyes watching me from the walls. The heads of various game animals were displayed in his living room, mounted over the couch.

I hurried into the bedroom, not wanting to make eye contact with the poor bastards.

Like the rest of the cabin, the room was furnished with the basics: a dresser, a king-size bed, a nightstand with a lamp made of deer skin and antlers.

The hunting trophies didn't surprise me one bit. What threw me for a loop was the bookcase nestled against the wall, every inch of shelf space accounted for with well-read books. The silver wolf liked to read?

Most of the books were horror titles. *Salem's Lot* by Stephen King must have been his current read since it was perched on his nightstand with one of the corners dogeared. Of course, he'd forgo an actual bookmark, the barbarian.

Setting my ax on top of his dresser, I dug out a flannel dress shirt from one of the drawers.

Was I really about to wear a dead man's shirt? Creepy, considering I'd beheaded him not an hour ago. But it felt less weird than wandering around his house in the buff.

I tugged the shirt on. It was practically a tent on me.

His dark and spicy aroma swaddled me, making the place between my thighs ache. Fuck, not this again. I was dangerously close to full-on heat, and my uterus hadn't gotten the memo that the silver wolf was dead.

I debated pulling the shirt off since the male's scent was affecting me in ways that made my core run hot, but then I dismissed the idea. The werewolves would have a tough time tracking me down if I smelled like one of their own. Covering myself in his scent would help my presence here go undetected.

I edged toward his bed. His scent was the strongest there.

Jesus fucking Christ. Was I really about to climb into his bed? I tried to rationalize the urge to roll around in his sheets as a survival move. But I knew it was more than that. My heat was right around the corner, and my hormones were going haywire, driving me to do unhinged shit.

Crawling under the quilt on the bed, I smashed my face into his pillow. I didn't want to be attracted to this male's scent.

He'd killed Hope.

He'd made me think he wanted me.

His wolf had told him to claim me when he'd already had a mate with a baby on the way.

That twisted bastard.

I was still crusted in his blood, staining his white sheets as I breathed in his scent, recalling the way he'd pinned me to that tree with the knife pressed to my pussy. His mouth on my throat, hot breath spilling over my skin.

Counting my piercings.

Teasing me.

Fucking me with his eyes.

My hand slipped beneath the blankets and found my center. My legs fell open, my fingers gliding through my folds and finding the last piercing he never reached. My lips parted with a moan as I pushed a finger inside my pussy and withdrew it to smear my slick juices over my clit.

I was so wet, soaking the silver wolf's sheets in a filthy cocktail of his blood and my arousal.

In the short time I'd known him, I'd hated him. Yet,

somehow, his scent clotting my lungs was like breathing in something warm and familiar. The memory of his touch would be branded on my skin forever.

"Fuck you..." My words came out fractured and breathless as I fucked myself with my fingers, picking up my pace. "Fuck you. Fuck you for making me want you."

My pinky finger hooked through the ring piercing my labia and tugged as I imagined it was the silver wolf pulling on it. I fantasized about his rough hands and sharp teeth working every inch of my flesh. Marking me. Making me his. Stretching my little body around his thick wolf cock, just like I suspected his beast had urged him to do.

I hated when Sawyer had hurt me several cycles back when he'd taken my heat as consent. The pain he'd inflicted was because he was a clumsy jackass who wouldn't know what foreplay was even if it bit him in the tail.

Something told me the silver wolf could've taught a master class in pleasurable pain.

My fingers plunged deep inside me, the friction making my toes curl and my back arch off the mattress.

My orgasm crashed over me like a tidal wave, leaving me gasping. I fell limp onto the wolf's pillows. Bitter shame washed over me as the afterglow fizzled, leaving me feeling small and pitiful in my enemy's bed.

I'd finger fucked myself to the memory of a mated male... a monster who'd killed my cousin and who knows how many other innocents.

His death should have made me happy.

I shouldn't have been touching myself to the thought of him. And I sure as shit shouldn't have been aching for him in a way that no amount of masturbation would alleviate.

CHAPTER
NINE

CARVER

"*Find her. Hunt her down. Don't let her get away.*"

My fists tightened on my steering wheel, my knuckles cracking and turning white.

My entire life, my wolf had never spoken to me. Now it wouldn't shut up. That rebellious bunny had awoken a primal hunger within me. It wanted her. It chose her.

"*She's our mate.*"

"Why her?" The monster inside me could have heard me even if I hadn't spoken out loud, but verbal responses felt better since I'd gone three decades without it responding to a single thought.

"*Because she's perfect.*"

"She's not fucking perfect." I was squeezing my truck's steering wheel so tightly now it groaned, threatening to break under my strength. "She's a rabbit shifter. Prey! Food! Our kind don't mate hers. She wouldn't survive it anyway."

"*With the way her cunt dripped at our touch? She was made for us.*"

It went on about how Ruth was our mate and how I

needed to let it out so it could track her down. I flipped on the stereo and cranked the volume up to drown out the voice in my head. Motörhead's "In the Name of Tragedy" filled the cab.

Catching the hint, it fell silent, and once again, my head felt like my own. But its words still bounced around in my skull.

Even if the rabbit shifter was my mate, it didn't matter. Even if she survived the coupling, my pack would see our bond as an abomination. They'd kill us both.

My wolf knew that, and it didn't care. It filled my head with the dark and disturbing things it wanted to do with her, consequences be damned.

Images of Ruth's naked body filled my head. Bent over in front of me, with her fluffy bunny tail quivering, my hands clenched around the base of her bunny ears as I shifted into my wolf form and forced her to take my knot.

My foot slammed on the brakes when a hulking shadow burst onto the road, a mass of muscle and fur bolting in front of my truck. The black wolf's eyes glowed in my headlights.

"Lila, what the hell?" Shifting the truck into park, I flung my door open and ran to my brother's mate. "You're not supposed to leave the woods in that form. What if a human drives past?"

I knew something was wrong as she shifted into her human form, her naked body stumbling toward me with her arms wrapped protectively around her belly. Her eyes were swollen with tears. In all the years I'd known Lila, I'd never seen her cry before.

"What's wrong? Is it the baby?"

It wasn't until her shivering form was in my arms that I realized she was covered in blood. A cold realization sunk in. It wasn't bunny blood… It was werewolf blood, and the scent was hauntingly familiar.

Lila was soaked in Casey's blood.

I took her by the shoulders and held her away from me to pin her with a wild look. "Where is Casey? What's happened?"

"We—" She visibly swallowed. "We found both of the female sacrifices."

My heart sank like a hot coal to the pit of my gut. "The girl with the purple streak in her hair, is she still alive?"

The concern in my voice had Lila's eyes widening. "Why do you care? She's a sacrifice. She's *supposed* to die. That's the truce, and she broke it by killing one of our own!"

"What the hell are you talking about?" A rabbit shifter couldn't kill a werewolf. It wasn't possible. It was like pitting a baby against a coked-up grizzly bear.

"Carver. Your brother is dead."

"What?" My voice sounded distant. Not my own. Lila frantically tried to tell me what had happened, but I could barely make out her words.

Casey was gone. Ruth killed him… *How?* How in the fuck did that little bunny take down one of the strongest males in the pack?

"If you'd listened to me, this wouldn't have happened."

I hated how right my wolf was. If I'd listened to it, Ruth would still be with me, and I'd still have a brother with breath in his lungs.

Lila's brows twisted with hate, and a fresh wave of angry tears rolled down her cheeks. "I have to kill her."

My wolf tensed inside me, and I pushed it back. "No. You have to go back to the pack house. Case would want you and his cub safe."

Bundling her up in my arms, I walked her over to my

truck, placed her into the driver's seat and handed her the keys. She hesitated before taking them. "I know you don't like participating in the Hunt. But just this time, will you do it? Will you track her down and kill the rabbit who killed Casey?"

Right then, my sister-in-law could have asked me to crawl up into the goddamn sky and wrestle the moon down for her, and I'd do it. Anything for the last piece of my brother that I had.

"I'll do it."

Every sinew in my body tensed, waiting for the beast inside me to protest. But it was eerily quiet, and that unsettled me more than anything else.

"Thank you, Carv. I hate to ask so much of you, but could you—" Lila's voice wavered and cracked, and she had to take a moment to gather herself. "Could you go back to Case's body and bury his head? Lars won't like it, but I hate to think of the animals getting to it."

Every chord in my body stiffened, the hackles of the wolf inside me rising. "What do you mean, bury his head? I'm not going to sever my brother's fucking head, Lila."

The she-wolf's bottom lip trembled, and she scootched across the bench seat of my truck, gesturing to the space next to her. "You're going to want to sit down for this…"

With Lila's directions and my keen sense of smell, even in my human form, it didn't take long to find Casey's body. He was lying in a clearing not far from my cabin, where I often gathered wood. My stomach churned, seeing he'd shifted sometime after death. He looked so small, bathed in blood and moonlight, his severed head lying a few feet away from his body.

I hadn't believed my ears when Lila told me that the little rabbit shifter had cut off the head of a fully shifted werewolf. If it had been anyone else, I'd be impressed.

Instead, pure loathing raged through me like wildfire, turning every cell in my body to ash.

How had she done it? I'd taken her knife, which was now in the glove compartment of my truck. The details didn't matter so much, but they helped keep my mind off the fact that my brother was gone.

I had to find her.

"Let me out, I'll track her down quicker than you."

I didn't bother responding to the voice inside my head. I didn't trust it. I knew its game.

It believed Ruth was his mate. He'd want to keep her, mate her. Claim her. I could feel its hunger for her clawing at my insides, morphing into something that I wouldn't be able to hold back.

I had to find and kill her before I lost control of baser desires.

Picking up Case's head, I forced myself to look into the face that mirrored my own. I'd promised Lila I'd bury his head, but I couldn't do it now. So, I tucked him close to my chest, resolving to give him a proper burial later. It was against pack rules to bury our dead. It was tradition to leave the body in the woods to be reclaimed by our land. But Lila wanted Case's head to be safe from the animals, and I wasn't about to argue with her. If Lars had a problem with it, he could take it up with me. I almost wish the bastard would try me.

Ruth had laid a trail for me, drops of my brother's blood leading me through the woods. The further away I got from where my brother lay dead, the thinner the trail got. Luckily, she'd come this way not even an hour ago, so her pheromones still clung to the air, making it easy to retrace her steps.

"Making it so easy for me, Little Bunny," I muttered, the inferno of desire and hatred spiking inside me as her scent grew stronger.

The image of my brother's body lying limp in the pool of his blood haunted me. We'd never go on another hunting trip, never share another smoke or beer. He'd never see his mate again or ever know his pup.

Grief morphed my anger into something lethal.

Something monstrous.

When I got my hands on Ruth, I'd make her fucking scream.

TEN

CARVER

Ruth's scent led me to the main road. She'd found the path that would have led her back to the main road, but she'd taken the wrong direction, which only led deeper into the woods—toward my cabin.

A disturbed smile split my lips. "We're really getting fucked by the fickle finger of fate today, aren't we Ruthless?"

I padded up to my home, sniffing out traces of the familiar scent lingering on the porch.

"She's inside," my wolf growled in my ear, confirming my suspicions.

Was she insane? Did she have a death wish?

Bunnies didn't have the same sense of smell as werewolves, but the place reeked of me. There was no chance she hadn't scented me. She'd had to have known this was my home.

"She doesn't know you have a twin," the wolf replied to my unspoken question. *"She thinks she killed you."*

I spat a curse under my breath. Ruth murdered Casey,

thinking it was me. Now, she thought the wolf's den was a safe haven.

She was about to find out how wrong she was.

Peering through the front window into the darkened living room to find it empty, I crept around the back of the cabin.

Nothing could have prepared me for the sight that met me through my bedroom window.

There she was, lying in the center of my bed with her hair spread across my pillow like a halo around her head. She wore a flannel shirt—*my* shirt—her small frame drowning in it.

Her legs were spread, the hem of my shirt riding up over her hips to expose her center. Slowly, her hand glided down the soft curve of her belly, fingers skimming through the trim little patch of pubic hairs. Her fingertips splayed, spreading her folds.

As she parted her pink pussy lips, a glint of silver caught my eye. A dainty ring decorated her labia. She tugged at it and bit her bottom lip, her face twisting with the sensation.

"My mate likes a little pain."

I hated the way my wolf seemed so pleased by this information. I hated even more that he called her his mate.

"She's the enemy," I whispered, unable to peel my eyes away from her beautiful body. "She needs to pay for what she did to Casey."

"Then we'll make her pay. We'll knot her. See how much she can take of my cock before she breaks."

My teeth ground together as my cock grew painfully hard. The beast inside me didn't want vengeance. All it wanted was her. Maybe he was the enemy, too.

Her fingers dipped into her pussy and, after a few pumps, pulled back out to smear her arousal over her clit.

My mouth watered, and I had to bite back a groan.

Fucking hell. Why did she have to be so damn sexy?

At that moment, as if some divine intervention was taking over, a gust of wind swept through Casey's hair, drawing my attention back to the fact that I had my brother's severed head clutched to my chest.

It didn't matter how beautiful this woman was or how much my wolf insisted she was my mate. She needed to die.

I staggered back from the window as my wolf suddenly sprung at me from inside, fighting for control. *"I won't let you kill her. She is mine."*

"You can get your dick wet once I'm done with her. Screw her corpse for all I care."

It was sad how many years I'd waited for the beast to acknowledge me, and now that it had, I felt cheated. It was supposed to be an ally, a friend, a source of strength. How could it be any of those things when the only thing we had in common was that we both craved this girl?

He wanted to make her his from the inside out, and I wanted to tear her open just to see the life bleed from her eyes.

Maybe that made me the real monster. I didn't care.

I watched the filthy little show she was putting on through the window for several more beats before stealing around to the front door and quietly letting myself inside. The hinges groaned softly, but the bunny's heated moans coming from the bedroom covered the noise.

I set Casey's head on the kitchen counter before grabbing the half-empty bottle of whiskey I kept on top of the fridge and knocking back a spicy mouthful.

My attention darted to Case, whose lifeless eyes watched me from beside the half-eaten loaf of Wonderbread I'd left out. The look of horror frozen on his face should have encouraged me to make good on all the dark thoughts storming my mind like a category-five hurricane. Instead, it felt like he was judging me for what I was about to do.

"She's just a rabbit shifter. You only saw them as food," I whispered to the dead man's head between shots of whiskey.

"All your brother did was what was instinctual to our kind. What you're planning on doing to her isn't fucking natural. It's twisted."

I scoffed at the wolf's words and stalked down the hallway, taking the alcohol with me as I quickly prowled toward my bedroom. Movement caught my attention from the corner of my eye, and I paused to examine my reflection in the circular mirror mounted on the wall.

Aside from the barbed wire tattoo on my face and all the ink covering the rest of my body, I looked just like my brother. Silver hair, strong jaw, hard nose, tall and imposing stature. But the pure loathing in my bloodshot eyes was all uniquely me. Casey never had that.

Lurking in the doorway to my bedroom, I watched Ruth writhe over my blood-stained sheets—my brother's blood.

I waited for her to notice she wasn't alone.

From this angle, I had a full view of her pretty pink cunt. She had three fingers stuffed into her hole to create her desired girth and still seemed to squirm with want.

"I could give her so much more."

I downed another swig of whiskey, sucking air through clenched teeth as the liquid fire burned me up, making my head swim and dulling the voice that told me to make her all mine.

As she came with a scream, her spine bowed back, and her toes dug into the sheets. Using her distraction, I stepped into the room and set the whiskey bottle down on the dresser.

My attention fell to the ax. *My* ax, the one I left in the area where I gathered firewood. The pieces fell into place. Ruth had found my ax and used it to murder Casey.

I ran a finger along the blade, hissing as the edge sliced into my flesh.

The blade was still wet with him.

The moment my blood hit the open air, the bunny froze in my bed. Her little nose twitched as she breathed in the fresh wave of my scent. Too fresh to belong to a dead man.

She bolted upright in my bed. When her gaze found mine through the darkness, her face drained of all color as if she was seeing a ghost. "No... You're dead. I–I killed you."

My mouth curved with a brutal grin that, to my satisfaction, had her flinching. "What were you thinking about just then, as you came all over your fingers?"

I strode to the foot of the bed. She scrambled away from me, her back slamming into the headboard with a clatter as the wood knocked against the wall.

Gripping the footboard, I leaned toward her. "Were you imagining me?"

She shook her head, and I barked an evil laugh. "Liar. Did you imagine my face like this? When I had your knife stuffed down your panties? Or did you imagine it covered in blood with the lights gone from my eyes?"

ELEVEN

RUTH

My brain reached for a logical explanation for all this. It drew a blank.

I'd murdered this son of a bitch. I'd watched the life drain from his eyes. I'd been there with his mate as she wailed his name and sobbed into the severed head clutched to his chest. Casey.

His name was Casey.

My heart squeezed, and there was a low flutter in my stomach. I stuffed the edge of his shirt between my legs to soak up the arousal dripping from my center. It didn't seem to matter that I'd just orgasmed. My body wanted more.

A perfectly built male wrapped in lean muscle and tattoos loomed over me with so much hate in his glare. Parts of him didn't seem to get the memo that I was the enemy. His cock was rock hard.

Carrots on a cracker. This bitch was huge.

If this was his smaller size—his poor mate. Sex with this guy couldn't be comfortable in either form.

The fact that he already had a mate and a dick big

enough to take out a few of my vital organs should have been enough to douse my lust.

Not to mention the fact that I killed him.

My uterus didn't seem to give two fucks. I was wetter than ever just at the sight of him.

I swallowed loudly and stuffed more of the shirt between my legs in an attempt to soak up my arousal that wouldn't stop dripping. "You're supposed to be dead."

Murderous red shadows roiled behind his eyes. "That's funny. So are you."

Outrage burned through me. "I never asked to be sacrificed."

"I didn't make the rules, Ruthless. Regardless, you broke them. Now it's time to pay."

My nerves launched into hyperdrive as I sat there, waiting for him to move. He didn't. Instead, he stood there, his eyes traveling down the length of my body.

His cock twitched in his pants, making my center thrum.

"What? Are you going to kill me?"

The wicked smile curving his lips was his only answer.

My heart hammered in my throat. "How are you going to do it?"

I was stalling. Trying to work out a plan. My attention flicked to the ax on the dresser.

He didn't seem to notice. He appeared to be too busy taking in the way my body looked in his shirt. "I haven't decided yet."

"Are you going to...?" Dread worked through my body, making every muscle in my body tight. "Rape me?"

His smile crumbled. "I'm no rapist."

"But you want me," I rasped. "In the woods, your wolf told you to mate me, didn't it?"

"My *wolf* wants you," he corrected me with a snarl. "Too bad for you that the part that wants you dead is in control right now."

He surged forward, and my survival instincts took over. I shot up from the bed and launched myself at the dresser, reaching for the ax.

My fingertips grazed the wooden handle before a large hand seized the back of my neck and threw me onto the bed.

The male was on top of me before I could scramble away. He shoved me down, my back flush with the mattress, and gripped my throat with both hands. Hunched over me, the moonlight from the window bathed his features in silver, lighting up his facial tattoos and the thick veins in his neck, swollen with tension.

He straddled me, his cock thickening against my belly as I struggled. "You look so beautiful with my hands around your pretty little throat."

"S—s—sick fuck," I wheezed against his death hold.

His breath came out in aggressive pants, his great chest heaving as his fingers tightened around my neck.

He was strangling me, and the more I fought him, the more he squeezed.

"Look at me, Little Bunny."

Gods. His voice was as deep as hell, full of malice and something else I didn't dare try to parse.

"Look at me! I want my brother's face to be the last thing you see before you take your last breath."

Of course. I felt so stupid. This wolf wasn't back from the dead. "Pro— Protecting my— Myself" was about all I could wheeze in explanation.

"You savaged him! You executed him in front of his pregnant mate. He was going to be a father."

I tried to scream, but I couldn't get a sound out past his vice-like fingers. Stars dotted my vision.

I kicked to no avail and clawed at the male's hands.

He bore down on top of me, his knees pinning my legs to keep them still. A complicated mix of lust and violence carved his expression into something truly savage. I knew his wolf was whispering to him, telling him to claim me just as it had in the woods.

We were born enemies, and yet the universe was playing some kind of sick joke on us.

It was said that when a shifter's deepest instincts choose a mate for life, there was nothing stronger than that bond.

But bunnies and wolves didn't belong together. We were doomed from the start.

"You want to know what my beast keeps whispering in my ear, over and over?"

It was like he could see my train of thought on my face.

"It's telling me to make you mine," he went on. "The fucker's been quiet all my damn life, but tonight he won't shut the fuck up. Maybe I should listen to him."

My eyes widened, and he laughed. "Maybe I should keep you forever by mounting you on my walls with the rest of my hunting trophies."

And it was with that diabolic line that the universe decided to deliver the punchline to the sick joke it was playing on us.

Because at that moment, I went into heat.

TWELVE

CARVER

*F**uck.*

The scent that bloomed from between her thighs was heavenly. She smelled good before, but now the aroma crawled into my nostrils and filled my lungs like a drug.

My wolf went rigid and eerily still for a moment. On the next beat of my heart, it was clawing at my insides, trying to take control.

"Fuuuuck. Smell that sweet, juicy pussy calling to me. Begging me to fill and knot it."

No. No. No.

I focused all my strength on keeping it together, pushing the monster back down.

This rabbit shifter had to be punished for what she'd taken from me.

Though, the instant I touched her, I knew I couldn't go through with strangling her. My wolf wouldn't let me. I was maintaining control, but the idea of killing her this way felt wrong.

Even with that slutty look on her face—her forehead

scrunched in pain and ecstasy, her eyes glazing with lust and hatred.

"Poor thing," I tutted in mock sympathy. "Your heat cycle is making you enjoy this."

I kept the cruel expression on my face like a mask. She couldn't know how much her scent was affecting me.

I'd scented plenty of she-wolves in heat before. This was different.

Bunny shifters had a reputation for being fervent breeders. The females often went into heat to attract a mate, although they didn't have things like mates—not the way we did. All that mattered was that they found a male to fill their little wombs and keep their burrows full of kits. Strength in numbers, that's how they survived.

They went into heat, and often.

I didn't think it would be anything like this. My mouth salivated. My cock was painfully hard, and I couldn't resist moving my hips to rub against her thigh. Even the barest friction was sweet relief.

The perfume bleeding from her cunt was more than good. It was a goddamn trap, a lure meant to ensnare me like *I* was the prey animal and not her.

The sheer look of horror on her face told me this wasn't orchestrated. She was more afraid than anything. The scent of fear was unmistakable underneath the heavy musk of a female in heat.

"Maybe there's a different way to punish her. She's so small. She'll probably break when we give her our knot."

Liquid fire tore through me at the wolf's suggestion. I shook my head. No, I knew what it was doing. It didn't give two bunny fucks about my revenge. It was trying to trick me into letting it out so it could mate and claim her.

"Come on," the beast crooned like a devil in my ear. *"Don't you want to make her scream?"*

Gritting my teeth, I tried to tighten my grip around her throat, but my fingers wouldn't move.

"I'm not going to let you kill her."

Fucking traitor. If I was going to make this bunny pay, I had to stay one step in front of the wolf.

Distant howls shook the night beyond my bedroom window.

That was it. My wolf might prevent me from ripping her throat open, but my pack mates wouldn't have that problem. Sending Ruth back into the woods would be her death sentence.

"No! They'll catch her heat scent before she reaches the road."

That was the point.

I shoved off the bed with a growl. "Get the fuck out."

Ruth sat up, rubbing her throat. I averted my eyes. The impression my hands left on her dainty throat did dark things to me.

"Wait. You're letting me go?"

My gaze drifted back to her. I couldn't help it.

Nestled there in the center of my huge bed, wearing nothing but my shirt and my brother's blood with the moon lighting up her hair like a halo, she looked like a dark angel sent straight from Hell.

The moment I laid eyes on her, I was damned.

How could something so small and fragile-looking crawl beneath my skin and hold my entire being captive? I had a heart of ice, and here she was, melting it with that flame in her eyes.

While the other sacrifices flocked to their doom with

complacency, she'd smuggled a knife into the woods and tried to cut my heart out.

She'd managed to run away, find my ax, and chop down one of the biggest males in the pack.

Sure, I hated her. But it was damn near impossible not to be impressed at the same time.

Case would've been impressed, too. Hell, he probably would've thought this whole thing was kind of funny.

"Yeah. I'm letting you go. Leave before I change my mind." I went to my dresser, where I'd left the bottle of whiskey and knocked back another shot.

Just like that, the atmosphere in the room transformed.

I felt her relax some now that she sensed that I wasn't going to kill her. But she didn't run. She remained where she was, nestled in the center of my bed, looking as though she belonged there.

"I can't leave..."

I stiffened and glanced at Ruth over my shoulder. My wolf believed she was my true mate, so instincts prevented me from killing her with my own hands. But she didn't know that. From her eyes, she'd nearly died. Now she didn't want to leave?

"This is the wolf's den, Bunny. You can't stay unless you want to be my dinner."

"Better than being ripped apart by the rest of your pack. Plus, I'm in heat. They might do worse than rip my throat out."

I turned around and leaned against my dresser to eye her on my bed. "You don't know that I won't do that too."

"If you were going to force yourself on me, you would have by now."

If only she knew the fucked up shit my wolf was thinking of doing to her.

I shrugged as I set down the alcohol and picked up a lighter and a pack of Marlboros from my dresser. Pulling a cigarette out with my teeth, I lit the tip, the cherry-red glow crackling as I took a drag. "You drive my wolf crazy. I don't know how long I can control it."

"All werewolves are supposed to have batshit instincts. It's the whole point of this stupid ritual, isn't it? Rabbit shifter blood sates you for the rest of the year."

"I've always had control over my beast. Well, until now. You're the only thing that makes it go wild. It hasn't even spoken to me until tonight."

Her doe-eyes widened. "Ever?"

I exhaled, smoke swirling around my head in a thick cloud. "Ever."

"So... what does that mean?"

"It means you've awakened something." My eyes drifted shut, and I breathed in the smoke, but it didn't mask her pheromones. The monster inside me lurked just beneath the surface, ready to act out all the dark thoughts shadowing my mind. "You'd better leave now before I shift."

"But..." She lifted her head, a frown on her face. "I'm in heat. There's no way your pack won't scent me now."

I nodded and took another puff of my cigarette in contemplation. "You're right. Your scent is just begging for any male within a mile radius to breed that little bunny womb of yours. And your dripping pussy will leave a trail."

My words had her lips parting with a breathy gasp.

I didn't miss the way she clenched her thighs and squirmed her hips, all while glaring daggers at me. Oh, she hated how much I was turning her on. Her line of sight dipped to the obvious bulge in my pants. She had to know the feeling was mutual.

"I have to wait for my heat to end. It will take three or four days."

I shook my head. "Well, you can't stay here."

Ruth swallowed, appearing to gather her courage to say the words burning on her tongue. "Why not? You've decided not to kill me, right?"

"I haven't decided fucking shit."

"Or maybe you *can't* kill me..." She climbed off the bed, heading for me. "Maybe your wolf won't let you since it seems to like me."

I growled at her in warning to keep her distance. The deep rumble froze her in her tracks but also seemed to make her pheromones spike in potency.

"She has to be so wet. So ready to take my cock. Ready to take my knot and every last drop of cum I pump into that tight little cunt."

She prowled forward, her eyes hooded and her steps purposeful. "Back in the woods, when you got pervy with my knife and decided to play your little counting game with my body jewelry... Your beast told you to claim me."

Every muscle in my body pulled taut as she approached.

"Your deepest instincts chose me. What if we really are true mates?"

My upper lip curled. "A wolf and a bunny can't be true mates. Shit like that only happens in books, baby."

"Guess you'd know." Her attention darted to my bookshelves and she looked back at me with a brow arched skeptically. "Do you actually read all these?"

My eyes narrowed. "Why else would they be here?"

I didn't like the casual shift in her demeanor. It was an act, and I knew it because her heart was beating hard enough to hear it across the room.

Picking her up and dumping her out on the lawn would

be the easiest way to get rid of her. But fuck me, I was curious to know what she was up to.

"You're a werewolf," she said with a shrug. "You're into guns and booze and flirting with your food only to mount their heads on your walls amongst the other innocent creatures in your collection. Books don't exactly fit that aesthetic."

"Pretty spot on for the rest of my pack. I'm a little different."

"What? Is this like the 'I'm not like other girls' trope?'" She picked up my current read on the nightstand, flipped through a few pages and put it back down with a snort. "You're special? Is that why you live way out here instead of in your pack's house?"

More like broken, but I didn't correct her. "My wolf doesn't crave bunny blood like my pack mates. That's why I don't participate in the Hunt. Which pisses the alpha off. In fact, I don't get along with anyone in my pack. So, I live out here."

"Why do you stay then?"

"My brother," I rasped.

"Oh... Shit. I'm—I'm sorry. I was just protecting myself. I didn't ask to be here, and I didn't ask to watch my cousin get torn apart."

"The blonde-haired girl?"

She nodded, her bottom lip trembling. "Yeah. I saw your brother and some of your pack mates kill my cousin. I ran, but... When I had no choice, I killed your brother. The way I see it, we're even."

"We're not even," I snarled. "There's a truce in place, and you broke it."

"What do you care about the truce? You said yourself

that you don't need rabbit shifter blood. You're different from your pack. You need something else."

I could see she was scraping up her courage as she stole closer to me, closing that precious distance between us.

With every step she took toward me, her scent grew in potency.

Was she trying to get me to shift? Of course... If we mated, her heat cycle would end. She'd be covered in my scent, which would allow her to sneak through the woods undetected by my pack.

Clever bunny.

"I know what you're up to, and it's not going to work," I growled.

Ruth inched even closer with an innocent smile cresting her perfect lips. I'd never seen a smile so fake. "And what am I up to?"

"You want me to fuck you so your heat will end. My cock is your ticket out of here."

"So what? You were gonna let me go anyway. This way, you get to mate a bunny. We're not just good at making babies, you know. We're really, *really* good at it."

She was dumping on the charm. Though, by her scent, she was inexperienced. I'd bet that worthless male she'd rode in with was the only partner she ever had. Not that it mattered to me.

"Wolves and bunnies don't mate. It's unnatural. It's—"

She closed the last stretch of distance between us and plucked my cigarette from my fingers. "Forbidden? A crime against nature? An abomination?"

Ruth put the cigarette to her mouth, and her thick lashes fluttered when the taste of my saliva hit her. She blew the smoke from her nose, reminding me of a bull—

especially with that septum piercing. "That makes it kind of hot, doesn't it?"

It did.

This whole situation was so wrong. She'd come here to die in some horrible ritual put in place by our ancestors hundreds of years ago. She'd nearly been ripped apart and instead killed my brother to save her own hide. Her pale skin was still crusted in his blood. If I mated her and the pack found out, I'd be disowned at best.

Fuck. That only made me want her more. And admittedly, I was getting tired of holding my wolf back.

"If you stay, if we do this, I won't be able to control my wolf. You'll be at its mercy."

Goosebumps pebbled her flesh, and her fake smile wavered. To bite her would mean to claim her. If she survived our mating, she'd be branded as mine forever. No matter how much distance she put between us, she'd always feel me. Maybe that was punishment enough.

Her eyes lit with determination, and she donned a deadly grin. With that, she leaned in and pressed the cigarette's burning tip to my chest. "Then *bite* me."

THIRTEEN

RUTH

I was drunk on a dangerous cocktail of this male's spicy scent, heat pheromones, and the instinctual urge to survive.

Okay, so maybe this wasn't the guy who'd ripped Hope apart. He still tried to kill me.

He could pretend it was all to avenge his brother, but there was still an instinctual part of him that wanted me dead. Wolves ate bunny rabbits, simple as that.

Even *if* his wolf chose me as his true mate, you couldn't ignore the natural order of things. He told me I was free to go, but the second I fled, I didn't trust him not to chase after me.

Then, there was the rest of his pack to worry about.

My heat pheromones put a target on my back.

If I could survive his claim, the urge to protect his mate would be stronger than his need to kill me. Then my heat would end, and his scent would cover my own.

Being the bonded mate to a murderous werewolf didn't sound like the world's smartest idea, but hey, it probably beat being dead. *Let's hope, anyway.*

I kept my expression sultry and my eyes full of challenge, daring his wolf to come out and play.

The scent of burnt flesh rose through the air, tangling with the smoke.

I'd expected his wolf to come exploding out when I'd burned his chest with his cigarette. But no, the male calmly plucked the cigarette butt from my fingertips and placed it in the ashtray on his dresser. Then he turned back, reaching for me.

I braced for him to hit me—to punish me for burning him. Instead, his palm brushed my cheek. He was hot, like a furnace. His thumb gently teased my septum piercing before sliding his hand back, his fingers tangling in my hair.

Jerking me toward him, the heat of his bare chest bled into my shirt, which was the only barrier between us. He angled my head back, forcing our eyes to meet.

"Foolish bunny. So eager to force my wolf out." His low chuckle scraped over my skin like sandpaper. "So eager for the beast to break you from the inside."

Fire ignited in my belly. "Your wolf won't hurt me. Not if it thinks I'm his mate."

The male arched his silver brows. "You so sure of that?"

No, I wasn't. But I couldn't let him know I was terrified out of my ever-loving mind. This was the best plan I had. It had to work. "Female bunny shifters are meant to be fucked hard and often."

"Sure. But they aren't built to take a cock half their size."

By his smirk, my eyes were probably fit to pop out of my head. "It can't be that big."

"Too big for your little cunt. You need to be trained to take me."

"I can take whatever you give me."

"I look forward to watching you try." He arched to kiss me, his lips searing against mine like a brand. I gasped against the shock of warmth, and in that same instant, my lips parted, allowing his tongue to thrust inside.

The acrid taste of tobacco was the first flavor to hit my tongue, followed by sweet whiskey and something else that was uniquely him. Smokey. Masculine. Angry. Like lust and damnation.

All in one electrifying kiss.

I didn't have a voice in my head like he did, but that animalistic urge was there, telling me to get closer.

My pussy was so soaked. I yelped in surprise when his free hand wedged between my thighs, his finger skimming up my inner leg to collect the arousal dripping down my flesh. He pulled back, popping the finger in his mouth to taste me.

His eyes darkened, and the tendons in his neck pulled tight as if his wolf was clawing at him from the inside, desperate to get out.

"You taste better than I could have ever imagined. If you knew the filthy shit the monster in my head is telling me to do to you—"

"What's it saying?"

The male's twisted smirk sent a shiver through me. "How it's going to eat your pussy until there's nothing left."

I couldn't hold back a whimper as his hand returned to my center, shoving between my legs and demanding entrance. "Come on, Little Bunny. Let me inside you…"

I swallowed thickly and obeyed, my stance spreading.

My cheeks—no, my entire body—flamed red hot as his index finger painted a soft, lingering stroke over my labia. Slowly, he pressed inside.

"Fuck..." I whispered under my breath, my legs starting to tremble as I spread around his thick index finger.

The wolf's steel gray eyes flicked up. "Scared?"

I shook my head even though it was a lie.

His smirk stretched wide. "Oh, Ruthless. You act so brave. I know you're terrified. You should be. I have no idea how I'm going to fit my wolf cock into this tiny little hole without ruining it."

I hated how well he could read me. I *was* terrified.

Here I was, about to sleep with a werewolf. Bunnies didn't bang wolves, and it wasn't just because we were natural enemies. The size difference was too much. Male werewolves were supposed to be huge. Too big for a female bunny shifter to fit, *especially* a shifted werewolf.

I talked a big game about being able to take him, but in all honesty, I just didn't know.

The most fucked up thing about it all was how badly my body burned for him. The size difference only seemed to make me slicker.

I could pretend I needed his mark to safely pass through the woods and that any attraction was only due to the crazy levels of bunny pheromones pumping into my system, scrambling my better judgment. But that would be a lie. There was a part of me that wanted him.

I liked pain, and this male would be sweet torment.

Reaching for the ax on the dresser, I held it up so he could see the blade glinting in the light pouring in through the window, still crusted in his brother's blood. "I wasn't afraid of your brother when I chopped him up with this ax. I'm not afraid of you either."

His arm snapped out, grabbing my throat. This time, though, he wasn't trying to wring the life from me. He wanted me alive so he could punish me for what I'd taken from him.

Snatching the ax from my grip, he pushed me, and I fell to the floor.

I made a squeak when he threw the ax down, and the blade lodged into the wooden floor between us, precious inches from my bare toes.

My gaze lifted to his. "What the fuck!"

The man lounged against his dresser. The moonlight from the window illuminated his face, the barbed wire tattoo stretching from each sharp edge of his jaw and following his silvery hairline, framing his features in a dark picture of deadly perfection.

His lips split with a diabolical grin as he pointed to the ax handle. "Ride it."

With the angle of the ax sticking out of the floor, I'd have to get on all fours and back myself onto it. Plus, the wolf blood had dribbled a little down the handle. "You can't be serious."

"Oh, I'm deadly serious, Ruthless. Ride the fucking ax."

He picked up the pack of Marlboros from his dresser, fished another cigarette out with his teeth, and lit it. His eyes blazed with the reflection of its tip. For a moment, he looked like the devil himself, dishing out my punishment for the murder I'd committed.

"Put on a good show for me, and I just might let my wolf out to claim you."

FOURTEEN

CARVER

"Look how beautiful she is on her hands and knees. She should be riding my cock, not that filthy ax."

"She'll take both," I muttered under my breath. She wouldn't have heard me talking to myself anyway. She was too busy trying to work herself onto the handle of my ax.

My wolf had woken up because of this woman. My plan worked—then it backfired. Now, I was torn down the middle. A part of me wanted to make her hurt for taking Case from me. The other side wanted to make her mine and never let her go.

She was so painfully beautiful and stupidly brave. Here was this sheltered rabbit shifter, who probably never wandered more than a few miles from her burrow her whole life, playing every shit hand the universe was throwing at her tonight.

I wanted her so fucking bad it hurt. It hurt almost as much as the thought of never seeing my brother again.

Without tearing my glare from her, I took the bottle of whiskey and knocked back a mouthful. The liquid tasted bitter this time, making me hiss as I gritted, "Lift my shirt up. I want to see you take it inside you."

She hesitated, her chin lifting as if waiting for me to change my mind. To tell her we could do this gently on the bed and that all she had to do was lay back, close her eyes, and wait for it to be over.

Too bad.

I wasn't going to make this easy for her.

I'd make her crawl for me. I'd make her body burn red with shame as I forced her to ride the weapon she'd used to rob me of my twin.

When it was clear I wouldn't be showing her any mercy, she drew in a breath and lifted my flannel to expose her plump round ass.

"Mount her. Rut her. Breed her."

"Shift into your half-form," I growled loud enough to make her jump, though that wasn't my intention. I was trying to drown out the voice in my head.

Her cheeks blazed with a delicious blush. "Why?"

"I've seen your ears. I want to see your tail, too."

The hate banked behind her eyes was so sharp I resisted the urge to flinch. Which had me smiling. "Go on, be a good little bun and obey your alpha."

"But you're not the pack alpha."

"Tonight, I'm your alpha."

At that, a fresh wave of sweet bunny pheromones flooded the air. Oh, she *liked* that.

On the next beat, she was shifting just enough for her floppy pierced bunny ears to push out from her dark locks, and a fluffy round tail appeared over the cleft of her ass cheeks.

"Now you're just torturing both of us."

Maybe. Maybe Ruth wasn't the only one I was punishing.

She reached behind her, her slender fingers curling around the shaft of the ax to line it up with her pussy.

"Those fingers should be wrapped around my shaft."

I placed the bottle back on the dresser, slamming it down a little too hard. Shit wasn't working anyway. I was all too sober.

The only thing I felt drunk on was my need to make this rabbit shifter scream and moan and gush for me.

I strode behind her to get a better view. As she sank the first inch of the ax inside her, her labia spread around the polished wood.

"That's a good girl. Your pussy lips look so good pursed around my ax. They'll look even better wrapped around my cock."

Any other woman would need lubricant to ride the tool, but female bunny shifters were supposed to produce extra slick juices, especially during heat cycles. A thick cream was already building, making it easier for her to take.

When she had a good few inches inside her, she stopped.

"You're not done," I growled down at her. "You can fit more."

"I–I can't..." she panted, peeking up at me over her shoulder.

"Well, then we're going to have a problem because my beast's cock is a lot bigger than that ax handle."

"But—"

"What happened to taking whatever I give you?" I asked, repeating her words in a mocking tone and snickering as her arms started to shake.

"That's not what I'm talking about," she snapped.

She craned her neck as far as she could to eye the wood penetrating her. Following her line of sight, I realized what she was talking about. She'd stopped short of where Casey's blood crusted the polished handle.

With a dark chuckle, I fell to my knees behind her and smacked her blood-splattered ass, enjoying the way the cotton-ball-like tail quivered. "You're already covered in Casey's blood. What's a little more?"

I expected her to be horrified by the notion of my dead brother's blood inside her. What threw me was how much wetter she'd gotten. Beads of arousal trailed down the handle, coating the ax head.

There was a part of her that was into this.

She gasped when I pinched her tail and tugged—guiding her back so the ax sunk deeper inside her. Her gasping melted into a string of moans and grunts. "Oh, *fuck*. This is so wrong."

I chuckled, my hand slipping from her tail to rub her ass cheek. "I'm going to have so much fun with you, Twisted Bunny."

Ruth's muscles tensed under my palm, but she leaned into my touch, pushing more of the handle inside her. When it was half inside her, she started to shake. "Th—there. That's as far as it will go."

"Good. Now fuck it."

Her intake of breath turned to a whimper. She pulled herself off the ax but didn't slide herself back down as if she was letting me appreciate just how wet she'd left the wood.

"That should be my shaft covered in her cream."

I had to fight my beast for supremacy. It wanted to shift, but she wasn't ready. It was too early in the night to break her just yet.

She wiggled her ass, giving her tail a little bounce. *Teasing* me.

A primal noise slipped from me, and I didn't miss the way her pale flesh pebbled with goosebumps. I gripped her soft tail again and tugged, guiding her back down on the ax.

Ruth hips writhed as she finally gave into the pleasure, her head tilting back as an animalistic noise wrenched from her throat. "P–please. Fuck me. Mark me."

"She begs so sweetly. Let me out. Let me claim my mate."

She glanced back at me, her heated expression full of need. For a moment, I allowed myself to pretend she wanted me—*really* wanted me. But beneath her seductive look, I saw her gears turning. Sure, she was in heat. But her every moan, her every word, was calculated.

"Please, alpha," she said with a purr. "Make me yours."

"Mine. Mine. Mine."

Shit. If I weren't careful, my beast would get attached. It didn't understand that she didn't really want to mate with a werewolf. All she wanted was to survive. After tonight, our bond would be a burden. She'd never be welcomed back in a burrow again. Her kind would shun her.

And it wouldn't matter how far apart we were. With my mark, Ruth would always feel me. The ghost of my touch would forever haunt her. She'd never feel pleasure again without thinking of me.

I gripped her by the hips and pulled her loose from the ax handle with a rousing *pop*. Before she could pick herself back up, I crawled on top of her and crushed her body to the floor beneath my weight. I took hold of both her ears and pulled, forcing her head up.

"You can beg and moan and bat your eyelashes all you want..." My free hand palmed her ass hard enough to squeeze a whimper from her. "I know that you're a murderous little whore."

"Fuck you," she huffed. She thrashed beneath me and tried to wiggle free even as the pheromones grew stronger.

"There's my ruthless bunny. I like you better when you struggle." I eased off her, giving her enough room to wiggle away. She took the cue and shot from under me. The bunny knew she needed me to survive but instincts to run kicked in before she could remind herself of her plan.

I slowly rose to my feet, laughing as I watched her dart from my bedroom.

The monster under my skin flexed as a fresh wave of her sweet scent washed over me. A savage smile split my lips as I charged after her. "Run all you'd like, Ruthless. I'll catch you. And when I do, I'm going to eat you."

FIFTEEN

Eat me?

If this male were anything other than a werewolf, I'd be game.

But this was a wolf, and I was a bunny. I could literally be game.

I bounded out of his room and through the darkness of his cabin.

For a tense second, I stared at the front door and considered making a break for it. A second later, I dismissed the instinct to run.

I needed his mark. I couldn't leave without it.

Besides, my heat cycle was making me want to play this twisted game of chase with the big bad wolf.

My eyes swept around his living room as I frantically searched for a hiding place. My heart bottomed out when my attention landed on the animal head trophies mounted to his wall, staring back at me as if in warning.

"What do you think of my collection?"

I whipped around to see the silver-haired male in his

bedroom doorway, leaning against the frame with his muscular arms folded over his now bare chest.

He'd stripped down to nothing but gray joggers.

He pushed off the door and prowled toward me. "Should I stuff and mount you among the rest of my kills?"

All sense of self-preservation was gone. Thrown out the window. Because fuck me, this man—this monster—was hot as Hell. Which was exactly where I'd be going, judging by the way my body was reacting to him.

I wanted to resist him. To get his mark without taking any pleasure from the act. Too bad there was no way of ignoring my pussy and the way it throbbed under his glare.

Spinning around, I fled into the kitchen. His heavy footsteps thundered through the room.

My feet froze in place when I spotted the severed head on the kitchen counter, blood oozing off the tile surface and dripping into a pool on the linoleum.

Fucking hell. I couldn't forget why I was here or the blood on my hands. I couldn't let myself believe for a second that I was safe with this male. Mates or not, I'd taken something from him I wouldn't ever be able to give back.

I managed to grab a knife from his knife block—it looked handmade. The wooden handle was created for larger hands, and the blade had weight to it.

With the knife raised, I whipped around, but he was there, grabbing my throat and forcing me to look at his twin's head.

Shifters often shifted back to the form they frequented the most in death. Casey had clearly been more man than wolf in his life since there was a human head on the counter instead of a wolf's.

"He's going to watch. Hope you don't mind."

Before I could fully process just how fucked up this all was, he shoved me back against the fridge.

I raised the knife again, but he plucked it from my hand and slammed it at my shoulder.

My eyes closed as I braced myself for the impact. A scream left me. Then, nothing. No stabbing sensation. No pain.

I cracked open an eyelid to see the knife protruding from the fridge. The only thing the blade had punctured was the shirt I wore—his shirt. He hadn't hurt me. All he'd done was pin me to the fridge.

I could probably slip out of the shirt—ancient instincts telling me to do what bunnies did best and run. But the heat radiating from his body threatened to burn me alive. I had to sate this discomfort.

So, when he bent down to press a kiss to the soft edge of my bunny ear and when he tongued one of my many piercings, I didn't fight him.

"So fucking beautiful..." he muttered into my ear, his voice crumbling under the wave of lust that threatened to drown us both. "So ruthless..."

He hated me for killing his brother, but I could feel his wolf gaining strength, lurking just beneath the surface of his tattooed skin. Something told me it didn't hate me as much as the man who served as its cage.

Earlier in the woods, it chose me for its mate, but maybe that was all a part of this sick game. Making me think I had a chance to live, only to tear me apart in the most brutal way a man could hurt a woman?

The silver-haired male stamped another kiss to the slender column of my neck, every muscle in my body winding tight when he trailed his mouth to my throat, his teeth grazing the sensitive patch of flesh.

It would be so easy for him to rip out my throat.

"You're shaking..." His growl was rough and deep, like sandpaper against my skin. I sucked in a breath as he slipped a hand under his shirt to palm my goosebump-covered breast. "Like a rabbit caught in a snare. You know what my instincts demand I do to prey caught in traps?"

A wicked feeling swirled in my chest, tight and confusing. "Eat."

"That's right, Ruthless."

He fell to his knees, kissing me down the length of my body, all while holding my glare. "I'm going to consume you until there's nothing left of you but a pool of blood and cum."

The closer he came to my apex, the more frantic his kisses became. Feral and hungry.

"You smell so fucking good."

My breath latched in my throat. His voice sounded different. It was deep and monstrous—wolfish. Only his growl wasn't that of a starving predator. His words were heated. Full of need.

I sucked down a gasp when he gripped my thighs and pulled them apart. He shoved his face between my legs, hot breath spilling over my center.

I hadn't had a man between my legs in a long time. The last one had been Sawyer, and that whole experience had been traumatizing.

As a bunny, I was supposed to like sex. I didn't. Just another reason why I didn't feel at home in the burrow.

It was like I was broken. Or, so I thought.

The moment his tongue slid through my folds, the pleasure winding through me was enough to make me see stars.

He felt good. More than good. There wasn't a word in

my vocabulary to describe how incredible his tongue felt, swirling teasing circles around my clit.

It wasn't just the heat. I'd been in heat when Sawyer had taken it upon himself to mate me. And that had felt wrong.

Getting tongue fucked by the enemy was screwed up, too, and in a way that somehow felt more right than Sawyer ever had.

This silver-haired male was scrambling my brain and my body, making my instincts go haywire. I wanted to run away from him as fast as I could, only so he could catch and claim me.

My thighs shook as his tongue pushed into my pussy. His fingers flexed tighter on my thighs, working with the knife to keep me upright because I was turning to putty in his hands.

"Sh—shift. I want to see your wolf."

He pulled his tongue from my pussy and sat back. My heart stuttered at the sight of his glistening lips wet with my juices.

He licked them as they curved into a savage grin. "You already saw it when you butchered my twin brother."

He wedged his hand between my soaking thighs and sunk two very thick fingers inside me. I was so wet that I took him easily, but the sudden stretching sensation as he forced my body to accommodate him had my head swimming.

Pushing his face back between my legs, he hooked his tooth on my labia piercing and pulled hard enough to wrench a pain-laced moan from my lips.

His cruel laugh sunk straight into me. "That's right. The little murderous whore likes a little pain with her pleasure, doesn't she?"

His breath washed over my center, wrapping around his fingers as they plunged into me.

He released my piercing and looked up to capture my gaze. His chest heaved with heavy breaths, and his pupils were blown wide with lust. "Answer my question, Ruthless."

The male wiggled the tip of a third finger inside me—a silent threat. "Answer me, or I'm gonna play a game to see just how much of me you can fit before you break."

I nodded frantically, the back of my skull bashing against the fridge. "I like it when it hurts."

His smile turned smug. "I figured as much. You put on such a pretty little show for me in my bed when you thought I was dead."

My breath froze in my lungs as realization bled in. He must have been spying on me through the window.

"That's right, Ruthless. I saw you rolling around in my sheets, finger fucking yourself. With Casey's blood still wet on your flesh."

His tone was husky and rough but not with anger. With *need.*

It was like there was some part of him that was turned on by the fact that I'd killed his brother.

My suspicion was confirmed when my attention dipped to watch his hand slip into the waistband of his sweats and fist his cock.

"Y–you're seriously fucked in the head. You know that?"

He chuckled as he pulled his fingers from my pussy, while keeping his other hand anchored to his dick and rose to his full height.

His hands slipped under my thighs and lifted me up the fridge. The sound of my shirt tearing free of the knife filled my ears as he lifted me off the ground. My legs instinctively banded around his hips.

My arms wrapped around his shoulders as he shifted my weight in his arms for a beat while he reached between us to tug his sweats down.

Everything in me went cold and hot again when he pushed me flush against the fridge and lined himself up with my pussy. "Of course, I'm fucked in the head. You think I don't know that? Look at me. I'm about to screw my brother's killer while his disembodied head watches from my kitchen counter. All because my wolf tells me that you're all that matters. How's that for fucked?"

The monster behind his eyes seemed to grow stronger, and for a moment, he went quiet. What was his wolf saying to him? I'd give anything to hear it speak again. Anything to see it shift and mark me...

"You're not the only one fighting a war. I want you, too. I want to mate you. *You.* The redneck loner wolf who tried to strangle me not even an hour ago."

He brought his forehead to rest against mine, making it so I couldn't look away. "I couldn't. I wouldn't. I fucking can't hurt you, not in any way that won't leave you moaning for more. Thank my wolf for that, Little Bunny."

"Let me see him," I panted, my hips bucking— desperate to take more of him inside me. "Shift. Please. I'm ready."

He bared his teeth, shooting me a manic smile through the dark. Fuck, he was so hot when he smiled. "No, you're not. First, we have to train that tight little pussy to take my wolf form."

Before the last words left his mouth, he slammed his hips forward, filling me with one harsh motion.

CHAPTER

SIXTEEN

CARVER

My little bunny's pussy was so wet, she was making a mess all over my cock.

Fuck. Everything from her smell to the kiss of her bare skin against mine was intoxicating. And she was *so* tight. Yet she stretched to take me with ease.

"Like she was made for us."

It took all my strength to keep the monster inside me locked in tight. It wanted out. Soon, I wouldn't be strong enough to keep it bridled. The deal was to give her my mark, and I'd need to shift to do that.

Not yet. My instincts would shove into the driver's seat the moment I shapeshifted. I wanted complete control over her in all my forms. I'd enjoy breaking and owning her pieces as a human and as a monster.

Primal instincts battled for supremacy, demanding I fill her with every drop of cum I had to give.

"Mark her. Breed her. Make her mine."

I gritted my teeth so hard that a splitting sensation shot through my skull. Being the demented fuck that I was, the pain made my dick swell—the perfect chaser to her inner walls clamping around me, sending shockwaves of pleasure straight to my balls.

She held onto me for dear life, her whole body shaking as I pulled out as suddenly as I'd filled her. An adorable whimper dropped her lips at the loss of me, and she arched her back off the fridge, her hips chasing me as I drew back.

"You love torturing me, don't you?" Her voice came out raspy under the layers of lust. "You fucking sadist."

"Sadomasochist," I corrected her with a dark smile. "I'm torturing us both."

"So long as you're in pain, too."

"Oh, you have no idea." Before she could respond, I pushed back into her. "I want to own every drop of you. Your blood. Your cum. Your piss. Your tears. I want to drown myself in you so I don't have to think about how incredibly *fucked* it is that I'm inside you."

Her eyes widened to the size of plates, and her pierced bunny ears twitched with every thrust I made. I was so attentive to her every move that I'd swear I'd be able to count every strand of hair that took flight in a breeze. I'd count every heartbeat from here to the world's end if it wouldn't drive me to insanity.

Everything about her held all my senses prisoner.

She wasn't supposed to be doing this to me.

I was supposed to be making her pay for Casey's death. Making her my prey.

Instead...I was becoming hers.

"This is my first heat of spring. I–I can't wait another fucking second. *Fuck* me." Desperation laced her pleas. Her fingers flexed, sharp nails digging into my shoulders hard enough to leave little crescents. I froze again, this time inside her.

Ruth cried out in frustration and fought me like the little brat she was. "Please!"

I gave a shake of my head and tutted as if I were admonishing a naughty pet. "Please, *what?*"

"Please. *Alpha.*"

Maybe it would have been my name she'd moaned on her lips instead of "Alpha," but it occurred to me that I hadn't given her my name yet. Had that been intentional? Perhaps a subconscious move on my part to keep a certain amount of distance between me and the girl I'd never see again come morning? A funny thought, considering I was sheathed inside her pussy.

In a way, I was glad I hadn't given her my name. I'd already told her I wasn't alpha or even beta; I was just some outcast loner of the pack.

She didn't seem to care. She needed my scent to buy her way out of the woods safely, so tonight, I was her alpha. And hearing her moan that title like it was the tastiest thing she ever had in her mouth had my heart aching.

Suddenly, I was all too aware of Casey's lifeless eyes burning into my back.

"What's wrong? Why did you stop?" Something almost akin to concern etched Ruth's features. The pang in my chest grew at her expression. She was beautiful, even wearing a glare, but when she looked at me like *this?* Like she actually wanted me?

It was fucking breathtaking.

And I couldn't take it.

It was a lie.

"Stop looking at me like that," I snarled.

"Like what? I—"

Before she could finish her sentence, my hand was around her windpipe.

"Damn. I love all your piercings, but I think my favorite piece of jewelry is my hand around your throat."

I expected her to fight back because that's what she did. That's all I knew her for. That's why I'd nicknamed her Ruthless. But she didn't struggle. Her pussy grew hotter. I felt a whimper catch in her throat beneath my palm—one of pleasure—and her legs tightened around my waist, drawing me deeper inside her.

I released a low shuddering groan as I fed her every inch I had to give in this form and leaned back just enough to take in the way she looked, pierced on my cock.

Her body was perfect. Smooth and tight, with soft curves begging to be mapped and memorized. The list of filthy things I wanted to do with her was so damn long, eternity wouldn't be enough to ruin her.

And all I had was a single goddamn night.

My train of thought started to trail in a concerning direction. I wanted her for more than a night. Because how in the hell was my wolf ever going to let her go once she had our mark?

But she couldn't stay here.

What choice did that leave me? Was I to follow her? Leave my home and pack? Leave Lila with my unborn nephew? For what? For a female bunny rabbit who only wanted my mark so she could live to see another day.

That's all this was. Survival.

My hand tightened around her throat, firm and hard, just like the strokes of my hips, as I started to punch into her again, invading her slowly, painfully, just like she was doing to me.

I'd fucked my share of unmated females in the pack. It was never serious, just meaningless ruts to pass the time and fill the lonely hours. Plus, every time my brother caught wind of it, he'd get off my back about finding a mate in hopes that the latest piece of tail would stick.

None of those past ruts had affected me like this. None of them had made me feel this fucking good.

"Because she's our mate."

I shook my head, losing myself in the pools of her eyes. "What in the ever-loving fuck are you doing to me, Ruthless?"

She laughed, but there was no humor to it—it was sharp and hysterical. "What am I doing to *you*? What are you doing to *me?*"

"Screwing your brains out," I huffed.

"No." Her face became stained with a bright red blush. "You're looking at me like a psychopath who plans to chop me up into little pieces after you're done nailing me."

I couldn't hold back a laugh. It must have rattled her from the inside because her face contorted with pleasure and frustration.

"That's rich, seeing as I'm not the one who's killed anyone with an ax tonight."

"Fuck you."

"That's all you got? No other bratty mouthed retorts?"

Her mouth opened, probably ready to fire off another snarky remark. I didn't give her the chance. My hips slammed into her, crushing her against the fridge. "I'm going to fuck you so deep, you're going to taste me, Little Bunny."

Hatred blazed behind her eyes, mixed with something brighter. Something that scared me more than her hating me ever could.

I released my grip on her throat, my hand dropping to her chest, ripping the flannel shirt open and sending buttons flying. I palmed her breast and plucked roughly at the loop adorning her nipple.

Her spine bowed against the refrigerator door in response, a smattering of goosebumps appearing on her exposed chest. I imagined what they'd feel like against my tongue, and before my brain could process what I was doing, I was arching down to take her nipple in my mouth and tongue her piercing.

My attention pinged up to watch her mouth flex with a silent moan. If I weren't already penetrating her, I'd stick my cock in that perfectly rounded "O" shape her plush lips formed.

Would she be gentle with it? Would she take her time? Would she cup my balls in her hand while her tongue traced the veins?

I wanted to explore and claim every orifice she had. I wanted to see my cum dripping from her every hole.

A dark thought fell over my mind like a storm cloud. Would I cum in her cunt? She was in heat, so it was possible she could become pregnant. A bunny shifter's chances were high.

She hadn't mentioned anything about protection. Then again, it wasn't exactly common knowledge that bunnies and wolves could breed.

For the longest time, we'd thought it wasn't possible. Then all that shit between the old alpha—Lars' father— and that one sacrifice went down.

Poor girl had been hunted down, but she hadn't been killed. Certain wolves liked playing with their food more than others.

There was no question after that.

The sacrifice had been put down before she could give

birth, so there was no telling what the child would have been. Bunny, werewolf or something in between.

All the more reason not to cum inside Ruth.

Not that my wolf would listen to reason. It had every intention of breeding her and didn't care that she was a bunny or that whatever child I put in her belly would be seen as an abomination in the eyes of every bunny burrow and wolfpack in the country.

The only thing it cared about was filling her womb.

"And you're going to let me do it too. You already made the deal with her to give her our mark. That means you have to let me out."

I didn't want to impregnate my brother's killer. But the monster inside me did... And I'd be powerless to stop it.

The dilemma had me pumping into her harder and chasing the pleasure to bury the rage building in my blood. I wasn't supposed to care about her. I was supposed to rut her hard, let my wolf do whatever he wanted with her, and throw her out in the morning.

Conflict, lust, and lingering grief from Casey's death had my brain short-circuiting. I buried myself in the moment, focusing on her and the feel of her hot cunt fluttering around my cock with every thrust.

Her lashes fluttered as I fucked into her, and sweet little mewls tumbled from her lips, making for the perfect distraction from the mire of my dark thoughts.

She was so sexy. So pissed off. So fucking turned on. It was a perfect cocktail that had me driving into her faster.

Those hate-filled eyes would set me on fire if they had the power. My ruthless bunny would turn me to ash given the chance, even as she begged for my mark, our bodies connected in no way a wolf and a bunny should ever be connected.

"Keep looking at me like that, and you're going to regret it," I snarled, my tone harsher than I expected. Guttural. Hungry. My beast was dangerously close to taking over, lurking beneath my surface.

I felt her sharp intake of breath down to the tip of my dick. "H–how am I looking at you?"

"Like you're a thirsty little cum slut with a chip on your shoulder."

My words created a visceral reaction inside her, and I could feel it. Her body was burning up around my cock, growing slicker.

As her arousal spiked, so did the hatred behind her eyes.

I wondered if she was thinking of all the ways she wanted to kill me. If my mating mark weren't a sure-fire way to sneak out of pack territory undetected, she'd probably take my ax to me.

My eyes locked onto the dark red flecks still smattering her face. Casey's blood.

I painted one slow stroke of my tongue from her temple to the corner of her mouth, tasting Ruth's salty sweat and the metallic zing of my brother's blood in one forbidden lick.

She turned her head to catch my lips, and the kiss sparked something to life, something primal that I couldn't shake, settling at the base of my brain.

The beast's guttural timbre from the dark of my mind spoke, his voice absolute like God speaking to me from the heavens.

"Breed her."

CHAPTER
SEVENTEEN
RUTH

A strangled cry clawed up my throat as the silver-haired man fucked me roughly against his fridge.

I tried not to look at the head on the counter.

They were identical twins, the same everything except Casey didn't have all the facial tattoos his brother did.

My heart was beating so fast it could explode from my chest any second. My mouth opened to gulp down the precious air he was stealing from my lungs. He took the opening, shoving his tongue inside me and invading yet another part of me.

He feasted on my mouth and swallowed every whimpering moan he knocked from me with each punishing thrust of his hips. His cock was much larger than Sawyer's, making me feel so full. How was I going to take him when he shifted?

Maybe I wouldn't survive it at all. But hey, getting taken out by a giant cock had to be the best way a sacrifice ever went out on Hunt night.

I could sense the monster inside him, waiting to pounce.

Closing my eyes, I imagined the face of the silver wolf I'd murdered in the woods, those storm-gray eyes staring into me in shock as I slammed the ax onto his neck.

A chill settled below my skin, which almost felt good compared to the inferno of heat building between my legs.

I opened my eyes to find those same storm-gray eyes staring at me from the counter. I looked back at the male fucking me. Those damn eyes.

I buried my face into his neck to escape their glare. Maybe it was too intimate of a gesture because his hand gripped the base of my bunny ears and gave me a rough shake, forcing my attention back on him. "Look your alpha in the eyes while he's fucking you."

"You're crushing my tail against the fridge. It hurts and not in a fun way," I blurted, the first thing coming to mind, bearing a tinge of truth. "Can we take this out of the kitchen?"

Away from that damn head.

He seemed surprised, his hips freezing mid-thrust. His fingers unfurled from my ears, and with his dick still lodged inside me, he carried me to the living room.

"Not in here! The bedroom... Please." I didn't want to have sex with all the dead animals staring at me, either. Better to be surrounded by his book collection.

He halted his path to the couch, considering my request again. Then, to my relief, he turned and carried me into the bedroom.

Stepping over the ax, which was still lodged into the floor, he carefully pulled me off his cock to place me on the edge of the bed. I chewed my lip as he placed himself in front of me and slowly pushed his sweats all the way down. They fell to the floor, leaving him completely naked.

He was so beautiful it almost hurt to look at him. His

cock was thick, wrapped in a network of veins that gleamed in the light pouring in through the window—still wet with me.

A pleasing amount of muscle wrapped his otherwise lean frame, which flexed beneath his tatted skin with every movement.

Unable to resist, I reached for his cock. He snatched my wrist, pulling my hand away.

"Are we doing this or not?" I snapped at him, furious that he kept me at a distance.

"This is your last chance to turn back, Ruthless. If you want this to stop, we end this now. You can leave, and I swear on my parents' graves that I won't follow you."

I blinked up at him, waiting for the punchline to drop because he had to be joking. But by the stony look on his face, he was deadly serious.

My eyes narrowed in suspicion. "Why are you giving me an out? I thought the whole reason you agreed to this was because you wanted to punish me for axing your brother."

He cocked his head, a slow grin spreading his lips. There wasn't a trace of humor in that smile. I resisted the urge to flinch, refusing to give him the satisfaction.

"You said you were just protecting yourself. Yes, I want to hurt you for taking away the one person I cared about." He leaned forward, placing his hands on the bed to pin me with that cold glare that filled me with fire. "But if I fuck you, I *will* come inside you. And if I do that, there'll be consequences that I don't think even you deserve."

Of course, there'd be consequences. His mark on my flesh would be a permanent reminder of this night... And I'd never be welcomed back among my kind again. Okay, that last part didn't seem so bad. In fact, that was kind of a perk. "I'm not going back to my burrow if that's what you're talking about. Why would I go back to the people who liter-ally tossed me to the wolves?"

"That's not what I mean."

"What then? It's not like you can impregnate me. Wolves can't breed with bunnies."

He opened his mouth, but no words came. He closed it again, and his head bowed, silver hair falling into a screen over his face so I couldn't read his expression. "Even if I leave you alone, you'll always feel me. And I'll feel you. Every time you get so much as a scrape, a bruise, I'll know. I'll know when you're sleeping, I'll know when you're awake."

I snorted. "What, are you fucking Santa Clause now?"

"I'll know when you're touching yourself," he contin-ued, ignoring my snarky interjection. He gripped the base of his cock, giving it a slow pump. His hand slid easily over it, my arousal making for the perfect lube. "And you'll know when I do the same. If you ever take another mate... You'll feel my jealousy, too. Just enough to be left with that seed of worry, wondering if I'll track you down and murder your lover. How I'll take away someone you care for. Then—" His grin spread, which looked so evil framed by his barbed wire tattoo. "*Then*, we'll be even, Ruthless."

My jaw fell open in shock. He meant his words as a warning, but they sunk straight to my apex, making me so wet that I knew when I got up, there'd be an obvious wet spot in his sheets. No part of me should have wanted this asshole in my life after tonight. A small part of me, maybe a bigger part than I'd like to admit, wanted him to haunt the life I'd find once I escaped these woods.

I'd probably think of him anyway when I touched myself. I'd think of his silver hair and how it was gleaming in the moonlight right at this moment. The wolfish way he looked at me. How his gaze centered on my mouth and how whatever he was imagining doing to it had his cock twitching with a thick bead of pre-cum gathering at its tip. I licked my lips as I watched it ooze to the ground.

Even if he was a dangerous monster, and we had no business actually being together, I wanted to remember him. I wanted him to star in my nightmares. When I came from my own hand or a toy, I wanted him to fantasize about strangling the non-existent lover for touching his mate.

His mate.

I was done arguing with him. Done telling him that pretty much every fucked-up fiber of my being wanted this.

"I need your mark. That was the deal. Otherwise, my pheromones are too strong. I can't be in heat when I leave here. Your pack will find me..." My voice wavered and trailed off. They'd find me, and then I'd end up like Hope or Sarah. In pieces.

"I'll ruin you." A promise now, no longer a warning.

Every fucked-up fiber of my being wanted this. If we weren't in this situation, if I wasn't in heat... I'd still want him. I wanted the cocky, mean bastard because, underneath that steely demeanor, that dark smirk and that arctic glare was something *more*.

And whatever that was, I wanted to make it *mine*.

He wanted the same thing, too. At least some part of him did. I could practically taste it, making the air buzz. So why wasn't he shifting?

Something was holding him back.

I slipped off the mattress, ducked between his legs and grabbed for the ax—wrenching it from the floor. The handle was still slick with my juices and almost fell from my grip.

The silver wolf stood to his full height and turned, chuckling as he watched me fumble with the weapon. Then, something wild flickered in his eyes as I held the ax up between us. He knew exactly how dangerous I was with this thing.

I'd already ended his world with it.

"And what exactly are you planning on doing with that?"

"I don't have time for you and whatever is keeping you from fucking me. I'm not leaving here without your mark." I gestured to the mattress with a jab of the ax. "Get on the bed. Now."

CHAPTER

EIGHTEEN

CARVER

As a thirty-year-old hermit who'd lived in the woods his whole life, I didn't get out much. But I had my pleasures. The full moon cresting the tree tops in a starless sky and the wordless joy it brought my wolf. A ten-pointed stag roaming behind my cabin in the early morning, fog rolling in around it like a protective spell from the forest telling me to leave the rifle inside and just sip my coffee from my porch and enjoy the view. Getting my hands on the last book in a series that the author had taken a year to release and having the ending be just as good as I'd hoped.

But this rebellious little rabbit shifter wearing nothing but my shirt, with my ax in her hands and murder in her eyes? Top of the list.

"Stop looking at me like that! You know what I can do with this ax!"

I knew exactly how dangerous she was with that thing. She unnerved me with it, even after seeing her get down on all fours and fuck it.

Didn't change the fact that she'd taken my brother's life with it. She'd take mine, too, if pushed.

My dick was harder than ever, and my thoughts darkened with my smile. "You don't know what you're getting yourself into, girl."

I debated telling her the chances of her getting pregnant were high. Would she even believe me? She'd probably see it as me trying to get out of marking her.

"Just get on the bed," she demanded for a second time, her tone warning me that she wasn't going to stand here and argue with me.

I slowly put my hands up, palms raised to her in submission as I moved backward toward the bed, a smug grin on my face the entire time to show her she didn't rattle me even though that was a bald-faced lie. Everything about this woman shook me to my core.

When the back of my legs hit the bedframe, I dropped onto the bed and laid down with my back flat against the mattress and my feet planted on the ground.

Only when I was lying down did she move to me, careful to keep the ax in her hands even as she shuffled onto the bed with her knees on either side of my hips. She didn't trust me worth a damn. Good girl. Bunnies always had good survival instincts.

Every move she made was calculated as she mounted me, each visible sinew in her slight frame coiled like a goddamn snake, ready to strike if needed.

"What kind of freak gets a boner when a girl stands over him with an ax? You don't know what I'm about to do with this."

She positioned the ax so the blade pressed to my balls. "I could chop these off right now. I don't need you to have balls to sit on this cock and make you bite me."

I laughed, and her brow wrinkled in annoyance. "What's so funny?"

"I was stupid for thinking that male rabbit could ever be your mate. No rabbit shifter could handle a mouth like yours, Ruthless."

Her eyes narrowed into venomous slits. Wordlessly, she positioned herself over my pelvis, lining us up, keeping one hand on the ax while her other held my cock in place. As she moved, the ax shifted, and the blade sliced the first layer of my skin.

I hissed, and the monster inside me whined.

"She's so perfect. And all mine. Soon that pretty little pussy will be filled and bred. Imagine it. Her perfect body, round with my pup."

I didn't want to dwell on the image the wolf summoned to mind. I couldn't get attached.

"Too late."

Ruth lowered herself onto my shaft, and her face contorted as I stretched her. The copious amounts of pre-cum, along with some of the blood that leaked from my fresh cut, had me sliding into her tight body with ease.

The piercings in her bunny ears gleamed in the moonlight coming in through the window as her head tipped to the ceiling.

My attention dropped to watch her take me in, a sight that would be branded forever into my brain.

Ruth kept one hand tight on the ax with the blade perilously close to the base of my shaft with her other hand now braced against my chest as she pulled herself up—my dick coated in her arousal—then back down.

If only I could freeze the moment.

When I'd fucked her against the fridge, I'd been in

control. Now, she was the one dictating speed and depth. She was just as rough as I'd been.

She was hypnotic.

A smile curved my lips as I watched her take me, chasing her climax and alleviating the ache the heat instilled within her.

A blush bloomed across her cheeks when she caught me grinning wolfishly at her, and she shot me another glare through the darkened room. "You're not supposed to be enjoying this, you sick bastard."

"Would you enjoy yourself more if I acted like I wasn't?"

The bunny's blush deepened. "*No*. That's not what I meant. Just shift already so we can get this over with. It's your wolf's cock I need. This form is useless to me."

"You're sure not acting like you find it useless."

She gnashed her teeth, but the effect lost its bite as it crumbled into a moan. "Shift. Please. I want your wolf cock. I— I *need* it."

The emphasis she put on "need" had me wondering if she was referring to her escape plan requiring my mark or if there was some other part of her that yearned for me. A part that went deeper than her biological need to rut in her heat state.

"Come on my cock first. Do that for me, and I'll let my wolf out."

A snarl of pain ripped from my throat as she nudged the ax closer to my shaft, the blade slicing deeper into my skin. The scent of blood permeated the air, but it didn't slow her thrusts. She kept riding me even as she spilled my blood.

Fissures of pleasure and pain shredded my nerves. Thick beads of sweat rolled down the sides of my neck, soaking the sheets beneath me.

"Fuck," I groaned, my head rolling back into my pillow

as she rode my cock hard. Blood, cum, and sweat pooled where we were joined, making a wet slapping sound every time she brought herself down.

"Fucking—"

Clap.

"Shift—"

Clap.

"You brutal—"

Clap.

"Werewolf—"

Clap.

"Bastard!"

I cackled hysterically, my hands moving to grip her waist as she bobbed up and down on my body. She had been angry from the moment I'd laid my eyes on her. Understandably. She'd been dumped in the woods by her own people, left to fend for herself. And that's exactly what she was doing. Surviving even if the odds were stacked sky-high against her.

"Shift, or I'll gut you like I gutted your fucking brother."

Oh, no. She'd crossed a line with that one.

Keeping a hand anchored to her waist, my other found her throat. I wrenched her forward, forcing her spine to bend until her tits pressed against my chest and our barreling breaths entwined.

"Go ahead, kill me. Use my corpse to get off, if that's your thing. But good luck getting a dead man to mark you, baby girl."

Fucking this girl was like playing footsie with the grim reaper. Undeniably dangerous. Addicting, too, when near death felt this good.

She could wear that pissed-off expression all she wanted. She was enjoying this. Her pussy clamped around me like a vice, growing wetter with every pump, and the obscene sound of wet flesh against flesh growing louder.

Electric warmth wound tight in my belly as I watched her ride me.

I bucked my hips, fucking up into her as I dragged her back down on my cock. A delicious little moan dribbled from her lips. My fingers twitched around her throat, pulling her mouth to mine.

"Come for me, Bunny," I whispered against her.

"Alpha," she whimpered, the sound so small and etched with bliss. She had to be close. "I–I'm coming. You're going to stick to our deal and s–shift, I swear to— *Oh*—"

Her thighs quivered, and her stomach clenched as waves of pleasure visibly wracked her body. "Fu—ck." The word came out as a two-syllable groan on her tongue. She collapsed onto my chest in a boneless pile, her perfect tits pressed into my pectorals.

A raspy growl rumbled from my chest as I craned my head to look down at her. With how the blade was still nestled at my shaft's base, it cut deep into my skin, but I couldn't bring myself to care. Anything to look at her for just a few seconds longer.

My fingers combed through her locks, and I wound the section with the purple through it around my finger.

She finally pulled the ax away with a sigh and craned her head to look at the damage. All the color drained from her cheeks as she took in the amount of blood she'd shed over my sheets. "Oh *shit*. You've lost a lot of blood. I'm so sorry."

She was apologizing to me?

I wasn't sure if I wanted to laugh or cry or keep pounding into her to chase the release that was just within reach...

I resisted the urge to keep fucking her, and instead, I brushed the backs of my inked knuckles over the delicate column of her throat. She winced as I touched the bruises, and the knot between my lungs tightened, making every breath I took agony.

"Don't apologize."

Her gaze lifted to meet mine, those dark eyes peering at me through her thick lashes. "Why?"

"Because I don't think you're sorry for a second. Besides, if you're going to kill my own damn brother, break into my house and threaten to cut my balls off, you'd better *mean* it."

Ruth drew her arm back. I saw the slap coming, and I didn't stop it. The crisp smack of skin on skin sounded through my room, and as I blinked the stars away, I saw her reaching for the ax again.

There wasn't so much as a flicker of fear inside me until she brought the blade to her forearm.

"She's going to cut herself! Stop her!"

I reached for her, but the blade had already sliced through her skin. It wasn't deep, thankfully. Tossing the ax aside, she held her arm over my mouth and, with her free hand, shoved her fingers inside my mouth—prying my jaw open.

It would have been easy to fight her off. I didn't.

She was right, we had a deal, and it was time to hold up my end... Even if there was a part of me that wanted to protect her... from myself most of all.

I allowed her to wedge her fingers between my teeth and dribble her blood into my gaping mouth.

The taste of her was like a drug, shooting straight into my bloodstream. Oh, *gods.*

My head spun, and my entire body ached as monstrous

instincts clawed their way to the surface. I'd already made the first shift of the season, but this felt different. More significant.

More... *Feral.*

This was the first time where I felt like the kind of werewolf depicted in human movies—an uncontrollable, wild beast.

I was no longer in control of my urge to mate and breed and destroy.

I was a slave to it.

As I was shoved to the back of my consciousness, forced to watch from the backseat, the monster's voice was a practice purr in my ear. *"My turn. Time to show you how we treat our mate."*

NINETEEN

J ust as I'd hoped, the instant my blood touched the silver wolf's tongue, he lost his hold over his primal nature.

He was shape-shifting right before my eyes.

Any other bunny in my position would be terrified. But my survival instincts told me I needed his mark. A voice so small, like a breeze in the back of my brain, whispered to me, telling me this was right despite how wrong it all was.

It was unsettling at first, feeling him transform beneath me. Feeling his bones rack and fuse back together, stretching skin with tufts of fur rapidly forming into a thick and flouncy coat of silver.

In the woods, I'd gotten up close and personal with his brother. Well, not *this* close and personal, but near enough to the beast to slay it. There hadn't been a lot of time to stop and study his features. It was a giant silver wolf, and it wanted to kill me with his pregnant mate not far away. It's not like I was going to stop and take in his features.

Now that I had time to drink in every detail, this creature wasn't wolf or man—but something in between.

His chest was still its same shape, only more expansive, with the masculine contours of his postural and abdominal muscles covered in a thick dusting of fur.

His legs morphed into haunches tipped with huge paws in place of his feet, and his hands expanded, growing twice their size, his nails extending into black claws that stood out against his moon-pale coat.

His head took on the shape of a wolf's—giant snout and a mouthful of deadly teeth—and had the little hairs on my rabbit tail quivering.

I braced my hands against his chest for purchase, my knees clamping tight around his hips as I held on for dear life through his shift.

At that moment, I realized my mistake.

He was still inside me, and if he was big before, he was freaking huge now.

It was too late to change my mind. Not after the lengths I'd gone to get to this point.

His cock and the shape it took on had my eyes crossing and drool trickling from the corners of my mouth.

He was longer, thicker, with maybe a tapered tip. It was tough to tell with how deep it was seated inside me. By the ridges rubbing my inner walls, it was definitely ribbed.

I knew the shift was over when the silver wolf collapsed back into the mattress with a pained growl that turned to a relieved purr on the next breath.

All the oxygen emptied from my lungs when our eyes locked. It was like I was looking at the ghost of the monster whose life I'd taken.

My jaw set as guilt crept into my chest, penetrating my armor of fury and vengeance.

None of this was fair. What had I done to get this dicked over by the universe? I didn't ask to be born into what was basically a cult, where young rabbit shifters were sacrificed at random to the local werewolf pack. Where my sister, my cousin, and so many of my kin went to their deaths.

I refused to conform. I refused to just lay down and accept my fate. As much as I hated to admit it, the silver wolf was right. I had *nothing* to apologize for.

I'd been forced into being prey and I'd turned out the predator instead.

The werewolf's post-shift haze seemed to dissipate, and he reached for me. I moved faster than him, grabbing for the ax.

He didn't move to stop me. He only smiled. At least, that's what it looked like he was doing. The human expression seemed out of place on his muzzle.

"It's only been one night since I've known you, but I've waited my whole life to meet you, Little One."

I stared blankly at the beast whose voice was raspy, low and full of growl. Summoning a coherent thought was difficult enough, with the gigantic wolf cock splitting me open, but this sudden shift in his demeanor had me turning to liquid. "Um..."

"So beautiful..." He tucked a rogue lock of my hair behind my ear with one of his massive claws, the simple motion shockingly gentle. "Especially when you have murder in your eyes."

The monster's words disarmed me. I wasn't sure what I'd been expecting when I finally met the silver wolf's inner beast, but it wasn't this. He seemed...kind. The adoration warming his eyes terrified me more than the cruel touch of his human counterpart.

Trusting the kindness bank in his gaze, I dropped my grip on the ax for good. "I need your mark, Alpha. So, let's just get this over quickly."

He laughed as if I'd told some hilarious joke. "Oh, Little One. You're seriously mistaken if you think this is going to be quick. We're together. True mates united. Tonight, we bond. Our first rut must be savored."

"I'm not your true mate. At least, I don't think. You said so yourself; rabbits and wolves can't be mates."

"My human host said that, and he's foolish. Blinded by the loss of his kin. Regardless, you will bear my mark. Therefore, you'll be mine."

"Technically, y–yes," I hedged. It was nearly impossible to articulate, considering how we were joined. "I'm only doing this to end my heat cycle and cover my scent. Your mark means I can leave these woods safely. Your pack is still out there, hunting me."

"You aren't going anywhere without me after tonight, Little Bunny. You are mine."

"Stop saying that!" Panic struck my chest like a bolt of lightning. Adrenaline coursed through me, making my body shake, and my breath come out in short, rattling pants. Just about every instinct in my body urged me to flee, but there was no running now. I was still mounted over his pelvis with his cock lodged deep inside me. "You agreed—"

The rest of my sentence was replaced with a yelp as his claws found my waist, plucked me off his cock with an embarrassing wet sound and flipped me over so that my back was to the mattress with the silver wolf looming over me, caging me to the bed.

"You are mine!" he repeated, this time with a roar that had my head swimming.

His paws closed around my thighs, his claws so large the tips met, and he pried my legs apart. My eyes nearly popped out of my head when I saw what had been inside me.

There, taking up an alarming amount of my vision, was an erect cock so huge and obscene that it was a wonder how it fit inside me.

A rope of milky white pre-cum oozed from the tapered tip and dribbled down the bright red shaft. At its base was a large bulge. What on earth was that for? There was no way something that bulbous could fit into a female, even a werewolf female.

The wolf's silvery eyes turned dark as his pupils dilated. He crouched between the crux of my thighs and, to my horror, pressed his snout to my pussy and inhaled. The masculine groan he released reverberated against me, sending shock waves through my body. "You smell incredible. Your womb begs for my seed."

I squirmed against the bed, but one paw lifted from my thigh, his palm flattening against my belly to keep me still. His other paw lifted my leg in the air to spread me wider.

The wolf leaned closer, each huff of his molten breath a palpable caress over my core.

A tiny little *"Oh"* left me when he parted his jaws to reveal the biggest tongue I'd ever seen, snaking toward my exposed center.

My heart slammed against my ribs in a painful tempo as deadly jaws drifted closer to my most delicate parts, his teeth gleaming wickedly in the moonlight filtering through the window.

A throaty mewl climbed up my throat with the first lick he painted through my folds.

He tasted all of me, from my clit to the tight ring of muscle in my rear. The tip of his tongue flicked the ring decorating my labia, and he reared back with a growl.

"It's silver!"

I gaped at him through the dark, my brain taking a beat

to make sense of what just happened. Before his tongue slithered back into his maw, I noticed the scorch where the metal had burned him.

He'd already touched the piercing, but that was in his human form.

The Elders always told us that werewolves' weakness to silver was made up by Hollywood. Did they really not know? Or had they lied to us to make sure the sacrifices didn't go into the Hunt prepared?

My anger devolved into panic when the wolf took me in his claws. A scream caught in my throat as I waited for the pain to register. A brief pinching was the only sensation I felt.

I blinked down to see him carefully prying the hoop open. With great care, he slid it off and tossed it away with an offended snarl. "What about the rest?"

The beast wearily eyed the jewelry in my ears.

"Surgical steel," I assured him. "Only that one was sterling."

He grunted in understanding and returned his tongue to my center. My hands flew to his massive head, curling into his fur as his tongue pushed into my entrance. He didn't fill me up as much as his cock, but it was wetter and more agile in the way that he hit my insides.

He plunged the muscle inside me, fucking me with his tongue until my body felt like jelly, and another climax threatened to swallow me.

The tip of his tongue curled, hitting a secret spot inside, sending me hurtling over the edge.

The beast kept me pinned to the bed as I screamed my release then he sat back on his haunches, his nostrils flaring when we locked eyes.

My chest heaved with my labored breaths, and for an intense minute, he just *stared* at me.

I was probably wearing a look fitting a bunny about to get fucked by a wolf several times her size. His gaze softened, and his grip on me turned into something tender.

The wolf was massive and scary, just like his brother had been. But there was that look in this one's eyes that Casey hadn't had. Something softer, meant only for a mate.

A flutter filled my chest as I deciphered that gleam in his frost-colored orbs.

Adoration.

"I'm not going to hurt you, Little Bunny." His purr was soft and comforting, making my muscles ease. "I'll give you what you need and so much more."

I'd heard that werewolf's beast forms almost had their own personalities separate from their human counterparts. What I hadn't expected was how different the beast would be. This one was tender in the way it held me. Careful.

Who could have guessed that the monster was the sweet one?

"I— I don't need anything from you except your mark, thanks."

Chuckling, the beast gripped his ribbed flesh and gave it a slow pump. He ran his thumb over the head and shivered when he dipped the tip of his claw into the slit—which pushed out another tear of pre-cum.

He canted his hips and lined up the pointed tip of his cock with my center. "Oh, sweet mate. You're going to take everything I give you."

TWENTY

RUTH

The silver wolf's body heat enveloped me like a fever. He arched over me, his tongue lapping up a drop of sweat. A hum rumbled from his chest as if pleased by the taste.

"I'm going to come inside you, Mate." His tone took a dark bend. "Every drop I have to give, you'll take until you think you can't hold any more. I'm going to come until you're swollen with me."

My face torched at his words.

"You're not to spill a drop. Understand?"

I nodded, and he purred in approval. "Good bunny."

My breath hitched as the head of his cock slid through my folds, teasing the sensitive nub of my clit. He pulled away, and a thick string of pre-cum trailed from his slit to mine. He found my entrance again and pushed inside, achingly slowly, talking to me in that husky voice while he fed himself to me one inch at a time.

"So big..." I moaned, and he groaned as I clenched around him.

He thrust his hips, shoving the rest of him inside me

with one sharp motion. My arms banded around his shoulders, and my fingers spread over his coat to feel his muscles flex as he started to pump into me.

"My new mate takes me so well." His paw trailed up my stomach to palm my breast, his heavy brow contorting with pleasure. "Such tender insides."

This time, when he referred to me as his mate, I didn't correct him. I liked how the word sounded in his mouth. It sunk straight through me to settle at the place where we were connected.

He eased out, pulling another moan from me with the motion and hovered there with just the tip inside as he stared down at me with those heavy eyes. They were practically glowing now, a pale blue and flame-hot.

As I drowned in his gaze, a question that had been burning in the back of my brain bubbled to the surface. "Why me?"

He looked at me like it was a silly question. But I knew he understood what I was asking.

"You are a rabbit shifter. The moment you stepped into these woods, you were on pack territory. I couldn't stand the thought of my brothers and sisters tasting you first."

"Your brothers and sisters wouldn't want me for a mate, though. They'd just kill me."

He nuzzled the tip of his wet snout to my nose. "Yes, and what a waste that would be."

"You don't care that I killed your brother?"

"You took a family member from me." He growled again but I could almost hear the smile in it. His hand trailed down my body to rest on my stomach. "You can repay me by giving me another."

Unlike his human side, the wolf had no intention of letting me go after he gave me his mark. The panic from that knowledge devolved into something more primal. "But your pack—"

"I will leave the pack."

"With me?"

"Who else?"

"And what would we do? Get an apartment together? Get jobs? What would a life together even look like?"

It was a ridiculous thought, spending our lives together. A few minutes ago, the idea of seeing this man after tonight made my stomach churn. But he was different now, gentle yet possessive of me. Like all the fairytales of fated mates from books I'd read. Too bad this personality was caged inside an asshole.

"The details aren't important, Little One. All that matters is that we're together in a place where we will be safe to raise our cub."

I squirmed beneath his palm, which was unnaturally heavy on top of me, and he crushed me into the mattress. "Even if you could convince your human side to leave these woods with me, we're different species. You can't breed me. There won't be a cub."

His tongue moved along my jaw, then my throat and traced my collarbone, and I reveled in the texture of the hot, wet muscle. He's stopped pumping into me—and started licking me. It was weirdly sweet and adoring. Like he was trying to comfort me.

Eventually, he drew back to level me with a look that sent a chill up my spine. "You have it wrong. I can breed you."

"How do you know that?"

"I've seen it done before."

A pang pulled under my gut, making my stomach clench beneath his touch. "What do you mean?"

"A sacrifice from many years ago carried our last alpha's babe to full term."

The pang in my gut turned sharp and burrowed down to my marrow. "That's a lie. Every sacrifice my burrow has sent your pack you've killed and used their blood to sate your Hunger."

"One lived... For a time. She was hunted down by the old alpha and kept for his pleasure."

"That's *deplorable*. That poor woman." My tone was rife with distress, and the werewolf tried to lick me again to soothe me, but I cringed away.

I was more aware than ever that he was still inside me, hard as a rock. I hated myself for how much I still wanted him, how much my body craved him. Even after learning that he could impregnate me.

"It is deplorable," he agreed.

"Why didn't you do anything?"

"This was years ago..." The wolf's gaze hardened, turning icy. It was as if more of his human self was shining through and speaking his next words. "I was just a pup and hadn't even had my first shift yet. The pack didn't know the girl was still alive, either. The alpha kept her hidden inside his house. Once she was discovered, my father challenged him. My father died that night."

"I'm sorry..."

To my surprise, the silver wolf laughed, the sound starting in his body and ending up in mine. "Don't be sorry, Little Bunny. I will start a new family with you."

A potent cocktail of confusion, fear, and intrigue coursed through my veins. On the one hand, this male seemed to hate my guts, but as soon as he shifted, his entire demeanor changed.

He didn't want to simply fuck me; he really and truly wanted me to be his mate.

As different as we were, we had one thing in common: we were both at war with ourselves.

Part of me was like his human side. I also saw us as enemies. The other part of me felt like we really, really were meant for each other. Too bad there was no world where both of us could ever belong together.

I shoved him on his chest, trying to push him off while my pussy clenched and gripped him all the harder.

"What is the matter? You don't want to have my pup?"

"I don't know you. And look at you. You're a werewolf. We're not supposed to be together."

His laugh morphed into an indignant snort. "We are supposed to be together because I have decided you are mine. Nothing else matters."

Nothing else matters.

How could he say that so easily? Like this wasn't a clusterfuck of weird-as-freak circumstances and that we in no way belonged together. Yet he didn't seem to care two rabbit pellets about it.

He gripped the underside of my thigh with one hand while the other held my ankle high in the air, keeping me splayed open. He nudged his hips forward and pushed his cock deeper inside me.

"Tell you what. I'm feeling very generous tonight. I want my mate to be happy. There will be many more nights to come where I can breed this tight little cunt. So, for tonight, I will finish in another hole."

He resumed his rhythm, pumping inside me at a steady pace. His toothy smile turned wicked. "But soon you will take my knot."

"Your... Knot? What's that?" As soon as the question left

me, it dawned on me he was referring to the strange bulge at the base of his shaft. "Wait. I can't fit that inside me."

"You can and you will. But not tonight."

The notion of squeezing that inside me should have horrified me, but I was too wet, too caught up in the moment. Too turned on.

I relaxed back into the bed, and he purred in approval. "That's my good girl."

He dragged his tongue over my face and licked at the seam of my lips. His hips punched forward with a harder stroke than the others before it, and my mouth opened with a gasp. His tongue plunged inside, mimicking the motions of his cock. Fucking my throat and my pussy in perfect synchronicity.

He released his hold on my thigh to press his huge thumb to my clit, taking care to keep the deadly point of his claw away from the sensitive bud. He groaned when I clamped harder around him, my wetness coating the bright red flesh of his shaft in a creamy layer of arousal. The sight of it, plunging inside me again and again was obscene. Filthy. And fucking perfect.

I knew I'd be touching myself to the image again and again on lonely nights.

Pleasure mounted. My hips bucked, and my insides fluttered. An animalistic noise tore from my throat as yet another orgasm ravaged my system.

The wolf thrust inside me, once, twice more. His cock throbbed and heated, and I knew just how dangerously close he'd be behind me.

Would he have made good on his threat? A dark little part of me almost wished I had come after him just to see if he would.

As promised, he pulled out of me with a snarl and fisted

his cock. All it took was one more pump—copious amounts of cream coating his fingers as they slid along his shaft—before he unloaded with a roar.

Hot jets of milky cum spurted from his tip, coating my stomach and my breasts, and thick droplets peppered my hair.

Before either of us came down from the afterglow, he shoved back inside my pussy, his savage jaws closing around my throat. I screamed as his teeth punched into the delicate skin, biting me.

Making me his.

Forever.

TWENTY-ONE

CARVER

The moment my teeth punctured Ruth's delicate skin, the bond snapped into place, chaining us together forever.

I held her tight in my arms as her body stiffened and her muscles convulsed from the pain. She bit down on my arm, not to give me a mating mark—bunnies didn't do that—but to silence her screams. When she settled in my embrace, I finally unlatched from her.

Her eyes were puffy and tear-filled, but there was something else behind them that had my chest tight with emotion.

I stroked my paw over her head, my claws combing through her hair. "What a good mate you are. You took your alpha's cock so well. I can't wait to see how much of my cum your pretty little womb can hold."

I kept praising her. It was easy until she drifted to sleep in my embrace.

My human counterpart stirred in the back of my mind, making its discomfort known. *"You'll warm to her soon."*

He wanted the control back, but I stayed shifted for

several hours more, enjoying the control as well as not wanting to disturb Ruth while she slept. I was tired, too, but I didn't want to fall asleep just yet. The moment I lowered my guard, I'd shift back.

The night eventually ebbed, and sunlight crept through the bedroom window. I turned to see where Ruth was positioned in my arms, a sunbeam wrapping her all in gold. She'd managed to keep up her half-shifted state even in her sleep. I envied that.

I stroked her bunny ear, loving the feel of her down-soft fur. At some point, I fell asleep, and as darkness closed in, I realized my mistake. With my last coherent thought, I hoped like hell that my human had come to his senses.

THE SIGHT of her tucked against my side, snoring softly into the crook of my arm, felt so...

Shit. I didn't know how to feel. The clusterfuck of emotions knotting in my chest was impossible to untangle.

Shifting her gently out of my arms, I climbed out of bed, careful not to jostle the mattress and tugged on the sweats I'd left on the floor beside the ax. I eyed it for a moment before trudging out of the room.

The clock mounted on the wall of my living room read 7:37 a.m. I plucked a cigarette from the pack lying on the side table along with a lighter and went outside to smoke my breakfast.

Leaning against my porch railing and staring into the treeline, bitter thoughts knotted in my chest at the image of my brother's dead body lying in the woods. It was pack tradition to allow our dead to be reclaimed by the forest, but letting the wildlife eat away at him didn't sit right with me.

At least I could bury his head.

After several more moments of silence, I decided to do just that. Going inside, I gathered his head then went to my shed out back and found an old shovel. I dug a hole not far from the cabin, placed the head at the bottom of the pit, and said a silent goodbye to my twin before filling in the hole.

My thoughts drifted to Ruth.

"Have you forgiven her?"

The voice in my head startled me.

"Oh, you're awake. You know, it's fucking sad how desperate I was for you to talk to me my whole life. Now, all I want is for you to stay asleep," I snapped.

"Then you're in luck because now I must rest. But soon, I will come out and claim my pretty mate all over again. Next time I'll come inside her. I want to see her drip with me."

The voice faded, and just as it promised, it drifted to sleep, leaving my brain quiet.

I finished burying Casey and went back inside, immersed in troubling thoughts.

My wolf wanted to keep Ruth forever. And that part of me, being completely feral, had fucking told her so.

She should have been mortified, questioning if I'd go back on our deal to let her go come morning. But she'd only moaned and wiggled those hips as I fucked into her. Getting wetter. Hotter. Like she couldn't get enough of the idea that our bond could be something more than a means for her survival.

I'd questioned if that tight pussy could take my wolf form. I thought she'd break, and I'd be lying if there wasn't a wicked little part of me that almost wished that she had.

But no, she'd taken me so perfectly.

The bunny looked so damn sexy speared on my cock. It was a miracle I hadn't come from that pretty picture alone.

"Do you think they found Sawyer yet?"

I turned to find Ruth in the doorway. She was quiet when she wanted to be. I hadn't heard her open the door.

My eyes dipped down her body, appreciating the view. She'd found a fresh flannel shirt of mine. She hadn't bothered with anything else, not when she'd just shift the moment we said our goodbyes.

"That the male you came in with?"

She bit her bottom lip. "Yeah."

My brows furrowed as I sensed the cloud of discomfort hanging over her head. With our new bond, I could feel her in ways I'd never felt anyone before. She was easier to read now, and the invisible anvil that pressed on her chest sat heavily on mine just the same.

"What did he do to you?"

Her eyes became slits. "I don't want to talk about him. He'll be dead soon, anyway, if he isn't already, so it doesn't matter."

I bristled at the sudden wall she erected between us, though I shouldn't have expected anything different.

A moment of awkward silence spanned between us. She ran a hand through her mess of hair. "So, are you back to being an asshole again?"

"*Mhm.*"

"Too bad. I prefer the hairy version. Better dick too."

"I was going to make you eggs and bacon for breakfast, but if you keep mouthing off, all you'll get is a throat full of cock."

Her bunny ears perked at the mention of food. It occurred to me that she had to be starving.

"When's the last time you ate?"

She shrugged. "I don't know. The morning they drew my name?"

Annoyance flared through me, though I wasn't sure if it was because she hadn't eaten in two days or that I cared at all. "They don't give you breakfast?"

She shrugged again as if going days without a proper meal was no big deal. "They used to feed the sacrifices but when the new alpha was appointed, he instructed our Elders to make the sacrifices fast once selected."

"Fucking Lars," I mumbled, turning around to dig through the fridge.

I felt her stare heavy on my back. "Who?"

"My pussy of an alpha. He's just as bad as his father— the piece of shit who impregnated that sacrifice."

"Your entire pack deserves to die for that…" Her voice was almost a growl.

"It was years ago," I said dryly. "But you're probably right. Except for Lila. She's probably the only one of us worth a damn."

Lounging against the counter, I motioned at Ruth. "Come here, Ruthless."

She hesitated for a beat before approaching me.

I reached for her throat, not missing the way her breath hitched. My brows furrowed as I took in the bruises I'd left. Then, my attention slipped to the silvery scar marring the side of her neck.

My mouth watered at the memory of her tiny body twitching as I'd made the bite. I quickly turned back to the bacon, pushing the dirty thought away with the menial task.

"So, uh, you said some pretty heavy stuff last night about keeping me here," Ruth said from behind me.

"My beast has a different idea of what this new mating bond means. It's sleeping now. You have time to eat before it wakes up."

"Then what?"

"Then you leave."

"Oh…"

Our bond was fresh and new. It demanded we be as close as possible. The mere idea of being apart felt wrong. I had no damn clue how we were going to deal with never seeing each other again.

That was a post-breakfast problem.

TWENTY-TWO

RUTH

My stomach grumbled at the scent of fried eggs filling the kitchen.

I sat at the tiny dining room table, marveling how this werewolf had come dangerously close to killing me last night, and now, here he was making me breakfast in nothing but sweatpants.

Ugh. Those freaking sweatpants.

When I woke up to find him in the kitchen, staring off into space, he must have been thinking about last night. His sweats did nothing to hide his hard-on.

And when he moved away from the stove, I just about swallowed my tongue. The turn he made for the fridge had the weight in his pants swinging. Yup, still hard.

His eyes flicked to mine, and his lips pressed into that smug smile. "There's a joke about sausage in here some-where." He opened the fridge and produced a package of meat. "But all I have is bacon, so... joke ruined, I guess."

I couldn't help but smirk.

He arched a silver brow in my direction. "What?"

"You're just..." I smoothed my hands over his dining

table with a sigh. "You're not what I expected. Like at all. Also, I'm a vegetarian."

He blinked. Once. Twice. Three times. Like I'd said something funny, and he was waiting for the punchline. "Vegetarian?"

By his reaction, you'd think I was speaking a different language.

"As in, I don't eat meat."

"Please tell me you're joking."

"Um, hello. I'm a rabbit shifter, remember? I've lived my whole life in a commune where we grow our own produce. And if we're feeling really spicy, we make our own granola. We're not into slaughtering innocent animals."

He snorted. "That's funny coming from you, Little Miss Ax Murderer."

My jaw set. "I said *innocent* animals. I'm sorry about your brother, but he sure as shit wasn't innocent."

Maybe it was the wrong thing to say, but being mated to this male had changed my feelings toward him.

I'd expected that on some level. What I didn't see coming was how close I'd feel to him. Even with his back turned and the two of us on opposite sides of the cabin.

I could practically feel his pulse and count each breath he sucked into his lungs. There wasn't just a physical connection, though. His emotions were right there, too, almost as recognizable as my own.

There was no trace of the hatred that had nearly choked the life from me last night.

I didn't hate him anymore, either. How could I?

I expected his wolf to be even more brutal than the rest of him. Instead, all I'd seen was a lonely monster who was kind and gentle in all the ways he needed to be.

The scent of something delicious ripped me from my

thoughts, and I lifted my eyes to see him placing a steaming plate piled high with pancakes and scrambled eggs on the side.

There was a moment where all I could do was stare at the steaming food, my mouth watering. "You made all this for me?"

"Can't let you starve, can I?"

"You could, though there are more efficient ways to kill a bunny. But I don't have to tell a wolf that."

Taking a seat at the small table across from me, he watched as I ate like it was the most interesting thing he'd ever seen.

"Um. You're kinda making it hard to chew. You're still looking at me like you want to eat me for breakfast."

He licked his lips. "I kind of do."

Fuck.

"I'm no longer in heat. And I have your mark. So..." We both wanted to fuck again, that was obvious. The sexual tension was thick enough to gag on. He kept staring at my mouth while licking his own. "There's no reason for us to have sex again."

His responding smile bore an evil bend, his lips peeling to reveal sharp teeth. "Who said anything about sex?"

"Oh, please." I rolled my eyes. "You're not going to hurt me. Your wolf is smitten with me. Anyway, you said yourself that you don't need bunny blood like your pack mates."

His icy eyes darkened. "No, but I bet tasting yours would give me a hard-on."

I brandished a smile as cold as his gaze. "You're disgusting."

He snorted, not buying it for a second. "If you're so repulsed by me, why are you fucking soaking?"

My thighs squeezed together, but there was no hiding

my scent—he knew how turned-on I was. "Look, can we cut the hate-boner banter? I'm going to eat these pancakes and jet."

"Where are you going to go?"

"I don't know. I can't go back home. Fuck those people."

"No family that you want to go back to?"

I stuffed another forkful of pancake into my mouth to cover the bitterness on my tongue. "My siblings deserve better. They're brainwashed into thinking this fucked up tradition is necessary to keep peace with the wolves."

Another stretch of silence settled before he hit me with another question. "So, are you going to tell me what that male rabbit did to you?"

My fork plunged into my scrambled eggs, and in a moment of rage, I imagined the fork going through Sawyer's eye socket instead. "I said I don't want to talk about it."

"He hurt you."

"What do you care?"

A vein jumped in his jaw. "I care because you care. We're bonded now. Like it or not, we're closer. Your hate is my hate. And I know you hate that male. I can almost fucking taste it, and I gotta say... I'm not enjoying the fact that it's washing away the taste of your pussy in my mouth."

His tone had my heart accelerating. He stamped a kiss to the pulse point below my jaw as if to calm it. "You're no one's prey, Rabbit."

His mouth crashed into mine, and this time, the kiss was different. "When you kiss me like that, I don't mind being your prey."

A low, delicious growl slipped from his mouth into mine. "Gods, don't tell me that..." He unbuttoned his flannel shirt—the only piece of clothing separating me from him. He bared my breasts, kissing each nipple gently before catching each one between his teeth and tugging on my piercings.

His lips continued their expedition down my body. Each kiss was slow, lingering and full of hunger. "I'll make good on all my threats to eat you..." Another kiss to my belly, then my pelvic bone. Lower and lower down my body with every kiss.

I tensed when he spread my legs, pressed his face between my thighs and slid his tongue through my folds. His eyes darted up, slit and blazing with something dark and possessive.

"I'll tongue fuck you into fucking oblivion."

TWENTY-THREE

RUTH

There was that smug-as-fuck smile again, oozing confidence and audacity. My thighs clenched again as a rush of warmth swept through my center.

Damn it. If he kept talking like that, he'd trigger another heat cycle.

His nostrils flared, and he opened his mouth, probably to comment on my body's reaction to him.

In a sad and juvenile attempt to distract him, I flipped him off with a grin. "Can you taste this?"

He moved so fast that there was no time to react. On one breath, I was spearing a piece of pancake and the next, I was being pulled from my chair, my plate crashing to the ground. By the time my brain caught up with what happened, I was already flat on my back against the table.

The male arched over me, his teeth and bright eyes an intense contrast with the shadows wrapping his face.

"Try that again, Ruthless..." He dropped lower to feather his lips over the new scar on my throat. "And you'll find yourself screaming on *my* middle finger."

The space between us was electric, with world-obliterating sexual tension and lust. "I think I'd prefer to finish breakfast with your other form. Something tells me the literal animal has better table manners."

"Careful, Ruthless." He dragged his tongue over the tender mark on my throat and chuckled roughly at the way I gasped at the sensation. It was like he'd created a whole new erogenous zone on my body, one that would only respond to him. "That part of me never wants to let you out of my sight again."

How would he react if I told him there was a part of me that wanted the same thing?

My eyes pinged between his, searching for more of that side of him that screamed for me to stay. "What's going to happen when it wakes up?"

"I might hunt you down," he answered candidly.

I glanced at the stuffed buck's head in his living room. "Like one of your hunting trophies?"

Something in his gaze softened. He stroked one of my bunny ears with strange reverence. "No. Not like one of them."

My need for him exploded tenfold, my legs parting wider for him in a silent invitation.

His thick tongue sunk inside me, and he swore when my walls fluttered around his invasion.

He feasted on me like a starving animal, lapping and sucking and thrusting into me with frantic motions. The wet, sloppy noises he made— like he didn't have a single fuck about how obscene of a show he was putting on between my legs.

I squirmed against the table, and a hand flattened over my belly to pin me down.

He lifted his face, licking his arousal-soaked lips. "Be still while I fucking eat."

My head fell back onto the table with a wisp of a groan as my goddamn soul left my body. His tongue felt *so* good. The pleasure drowned out the instinctual voice in my head, telling me it was wrong for prey to mate with its predator.

"Oh!" My back arched off the table as his tongue left me, only to be replaced with two fingers. His lips encircled my clit, his tongue flicking the tender bud.

"You squeeze me so tightly, Ruthless." The male's brow twisted as if he was drawing as much enjoyment from this as I was. "You're so fucking sexy. I want to have you for breakfast every morning."

The confession was the final push into mind-shattering ecstasy. I wanted to scream his name, but it dawned on me...

I still didn't know it.

"What's your name?"

The silver wolf stared at me for a tense moment before a smile broke out on his face. "It's Carver."

Carver? That name rang a bell somewhere in my head.

Why was it so familiar?

The thought fell away to the back of my mind as Carver's fingers curled inside me, pressing that deep place inside me that had me falling apart around him with a cry. "Oh, *fuck*."

My world spun again as he flipped me so I was on my stomach, bent over the table. His fingers plunged into my pussy and scooped my arousal out, smearing it over my asshole. His index finger circled the tight hole a few times before plunging one in. I gripped the edge of the table and gasped in shock.

"What? You didn't think I could leave this ass untouched for long, did you? All your holes are mine."

He withdrew his finger, and his cock pushed against the ring of muscle on the next breath. "Relax, baby..." he huffed, his face so close to my shoulder blades I could feel the caress of his breath. "You're choking my cock so fucking tight I can barely breathe."

"It hurts—" I was enjoying the way he was stretching me and the pain that came with it, but the edge in my tone had him softening.

Things really had shifted between us. Was his wolf whispering into his ear and changing his mind about me?

"You're doing so well, my dirty little bunny. Your little holes are so pretty when they stretch to take me."

He pulled out and plunged in again with a moan. "What a tight, slutty little body you have. The perfect cocksleeve."

His hands came to rest on either side of my head, his sharp nails digging marks into the wood.

"Oh, Carver. It feels so—"

His hand slapped over my mouth. "Shut up. Someone's coming."

The crunch of gravel crystalized the breath in my lungs. *Oh no.*

I expected Carver to pull out, but he kept pounding into me, chasing his release even as the truck engine was cut and the sound of footsteps came up the porch steps.

"Shit. It's my brother's mate."

My heart dropped to the pit of my stomach. I tried to get up, and the werewolf pushed me back down, whispering in my ear, "I'm not done with your cunt yet."

My heart slammed against the tabletop when a knock at the front door sounded.

Oh gods, oh gods. Would she hear us? The table creaked with Carver's movements, and his balls smacked against my pussy, loud enough for me to wonder if she'd hear it through the door.

"See what you're doing to me?" he hissed against the shell of my ear. "I can't stop fucking you. Not even when my brother's mourning mate is at my door, wondering if I've hunted you down yet. She asked me to avenge Casey, and look what I'm doing instead... I'm balls deep in his killer, with my mating claim on her whore throat."

I bit the inside of my arm to keep myself from crying out as his thrusts turned punishing.

"And you know the craziest thing?" he continued through his labored breaths. "I don't give a fuck. All I care about is easing this ache in my chest. It only goes away when I'm inside you."

I angled my head to watch him as he came. His face contorted with a silent cry, the devotion in his eyes completely unguarded.

His cock pulsed, and a wash of fluid filled me. I shivered, his cum spreading through me, thick and molten like honey.

"Carver!" Another series of heavy knocks. "Open the fucking door!"

It wasn't until he'd emptied his last drop into me that he pulled out and quickly stuffed himself back into his pants. Then he bent, swept my hair out of the way and planted a kiss so sweet to my nape that it left me boneless against the table.

"Hide. In my bedroom. And be quiet, please. I don't want to hurt her, but my wolf will do whatever it takes to protect you. So, please, for the sake of my unborn nephew."

I gaped at him, my head bobbing in a shocked and silent nod.

The urgency in his voice had my legs moving for the bedroom. The woman's muffled voice called for Carver again.

Then, it hit me like a brick of dynamite. I'd heard her say that name before when the black she-wolf and Casey found me in the woods.

We should give her to Carver, he likes the sassy ones. Like the purple-haired girl from last year. Called her tasty.

My knees nearly buckled, and my hand flung out to catch myself on the dresser. Was Carver the one who killed my sister? Had he torn her to shreds?

The scene I'd been suppressing... of watching my cousin be torn apart by wolves as I watched helplessly from the bushes forced itself into my mind. Only instead of Hope's face, it was Sarah's.

No. Carver said he never participated in the Hunt. But what else could Lila have meant?

...called her tasty.

That. Mother. Fucker.

The silver wolf—the male I'd be mated to until the day I died—was the wolf responsible for Sarah's death.

TWENTY-FOUR

CARVER

"Carver, answer the damn door!" Lila demanded from my front porch. She rattled the knob hard enough to tear it off. "Since when do you keep your front door locked?"

My attention zoned in on Lila's pregnant silhouette falling over the blinds.

If it was anyone else at my door, I wouldn't open it. But this was Lila.

"Fuck," I muttered beneath my breath as I approached. If she scented Ruth, shit would hit the fan. But I couldn't keep Lila locked out. She lost Case too.

I opened the door to find my twin's mate on my porch, her eyes swollen and bloodshot from crying, looking like a different woman than she'd been last night.

"Carv..." Her voice shook and threatened to crack. "Oh, Carver. I'm so sorry."

"Don't apologize, Lil. You didn't do anything wrong."

Her brows gnashed. "Like hell! I let that bitch get away! I should have gone after her."

My chest tightened with a complicated mess of emotions. "You did the right thing for the baby. Casey wouldn't have wanted either of you hurt."

"Yeah... Yeah, you're right. I keep trying to tell myself that." Her voice was raw and scratchy. Fresh tears started to spill down her cheeks before she quickly wiped them away with a swipe of her hand. "Anyway, I brought your truck back."

She held out the keys, and I took them with a weighted sigh. "You didn't have to do that. You should be back at the pack house, resting."

"I can't just sit around. Not when I know she's still out there."

Lila flicked her gaze toward the tree line, and I wished like hell the horrible feeling in my chest would go away. "Last night, you said you would join the Hunt." She whipped her attention back to me. "What happened to that?"

"I... I lost the girl's scent."

Lila's eyes narrowed, and the ache in my chest spread. "You're the best tracker in the pack."

"I'm the best *hunter*," I corrected. "Give me a gun, and I can feed the pack all year round. But you know I'm not the most potent in my wolf form. My wolf doesn't... Uh..." My hand rubbed the back of my skull. "My instincts don't really work the same way everyone else's does."

Lila frowned. "Yeah. Casey mentioned something about that before. Says your beast doesn't talk to you."

"It did last night."

"Oh?" It seemed like she wanted to follow that up with a congratulations but bit her tongue. Lila probably assumed my wolf spoke to me because of Casey's death. I didn't correct her—it was less complicated than the truth.

"Look. It's okay. We'll find her."

"Y–yeah."

"Lie better, or she'll know you're full of shit."

The wolf had awoken.

"I'll get my claws in her, Lil. I can promise you that." At least that wasn't a lie. "For now, you should go back to the pack house and get some sleep."

She nodded in agreement, and the next thing I knew, she was flinging herself into my arms.

Every muscle in my body tightened as she buried her face into my chest. I resisted the instinct to push her away before she picked up on Ruth's scent. Instead, I held her as she cried and waited patiently for her tears to subside.

After a few minutes, she pulled back, her nose wrinkling. "You smell weird."

My heart stalled out.

"It's probably just the pregnancy nose." She dismissed that with a sigh. Her attention flicked to the fresh dirt mound in my yard. "So, you buried his head?"

"Just like you asked."

"Thanks." Lila chewed her lip in thought. "Look. I should leave you alone to grieve and shit... But...I feel like this can't wait. Case was always on your ass about getting a mate and fitting in with the pack... And let's face it, none of the wolves in our pack are meant to be your mate. Maybe the one you're meant to be bonded with is in a different pack. I always got the feeling that the only reason you stuck around here was because of your brother."

It was true.

I fucking hated it here. I always had, even when our father was still alive.

"What are you getting at, Lil?"

"I don't want you to stay just because of me and the baby, alright?"

"Are you saying I should just abandon you and my nephew? You're my family."

"You aren't abandoning us. We'll still be family even if you leave, and you can always come back and visit."

She wouldn't feel that way if she knew what sins I'd committed last night. And this morning.

Guilt threaded through my system like poison, making me ache all over as Lila said her goodbyes, then shifted into her wolf form and disappeared into the woods.

I turned and headed back into the cabin, calling to my bunny. "You can come out now, Ruthless."

When there was no answer, I knew something was wrong.

I entered the bedroom and froze. Ruth's scent was faint, swept away by the breeze that flowed through the open window.

She left. Climbed out the window.

"No." My fists clenched into balls at my sides as rage built inside me.

I shouldn't have been surprised. This was what we'd agreed on, after all. Fuck like rabbits, create a mating bond to cover her scent and end her heat cycle. Never see each other again. But the moment I'd marked her, priorities had changed. She felt like mine.

"*She* is *mine*."

This time, I had no urge to resist the monster inside me. There was no fighting it anyway, not this time. Now I wanted what the beast did—her.

The shift came on without me even thinking about it. This pain was like an adrenaline shot, slamming through my system, heightening my excitement and making my heart pound. It was time to hunt, and the next time I caught her, she wouldn't escape me again.

Not ever.

TWENTY-FIVE

RUTH

I wove between the trees as fast as my little bunny feet could carry me. Now that it was daytime, the sunlight that managed to squeeze through the thick canopy of trees lit my path well enough, though it wasn't much help. I had no idea where I was going. It didn't matter. All I could think about was putting as much distance between me and my new mate as possible.

What had I done?

Allowing a *werewolf* to claim me had seemed like the only way to guarantee the safest escape possible. It had felt right for reasons that went beyond survival.

I stopped dead in my tracks when the breeze carried a new scent—the masculine fragrance of pine and smoke. Every hair on my tiny bunny body stood when I felt the scar on my throat throb.

I could feel his approach like a narcotic in my blood. The bastard was tailing me.

My heart raced as I lurched back into full speed, the cold knife of betrayal stabbing my lungs with every frantic breath I took.

I bet this whole thing was just a sick game to him. This had to have been his plan the entire time: give me hope of escape only to hunt me down.

He'd told me I wasn't like his other hunting trophies... Another lie.

I felt so fucking stupid. I'd actually started to form feelings for the fucker. Deep, complicated feelings that would sit with me forever. Feelings I couldn't shake even now, knowing what he did to my sister.

The mark on my throat blazed hotter the closer he came. Two instincts waged war inside me. A rabbit's instinct to run from the predator and the instinct to turn around and submit to my mate.

The snag of a branch had my beady eyes darting off my path ahead. I regretted looking. My thundering pulse nearly stopped when I registered two glowing eyes exploding from the bushes at my side. The pale-furred monster lunged, his jaws closing around my tiny body.

Teeth glinting, hot breath ruffled my fur and strings of saliva flecked my coat.

Before he could crush me in his maw, I shifted back to my human form and jerked my body away, rolling onto the forest floor. Twigs and stones sliced my skin, and the wolf behind me let loose a low growl the moment the scent of my blood hit the air.

"Fuck, you smell so goddamn good, Little Bunny."

"Get away from me!" I lurched to my feet and started to run, but he was too quick. He lunged again, and his giant arms ensnared my waist, taking us both to the ground.

The moment I was in his arms, an intense heat burst beneath my skin, sinking between my thighs. His claw-tipped paws clamped down on my hips, and he pulled me back.

"No!" My hands raked at the ground, dirt lodging beneath my nails as I tried to scramble away. "You said you'd let me go. That was the deal!"

"My human made you that deal. I'd never promise anything so stupid." His dark chuckle was all gravel. He rose on his knees as he positioned me so I was on all fours and draped his hulking form over my slight frame. "Now that you wear my mark, there's no escaping me."

"I'm not your prey!" I gasped against him. "You said so yourself."

His wet nose brushed the shell of my ear, making my skin prickle. "You're the one who wanted to play a game of wolf and rabbit, Little One."

He lifted one paw from my hip, trailing it up the curve of my waist and gripped my breast possessively. He plucked at the piercing hard enough to leave me gasping.

"I don't want this. I don't want you."

"Liar," he huffed, calling me out. "My mate's sweet cunt is dripping for me, begging for me to take it. Even if it wasn't, I can feel your emotions. Your resentment is threaded tight with lust."

He slid his tongue along the column of my neck and lapped gently at the mating mark on my throat.

The monster's fever-hot breath washed down my neck, and his dark and wild scent clotted my lungs. The feel of his soft fur against my naked skin was like a shock to my senses.

Despite how much my mind was against him, my body didn't care. These things just made my pussy wetter.

With his knee, he nudged my thighs apart, and his paw on my hip slipped around to cup the most intimate part of me.

I wanted to scream, but no sound came out.

My eyes shuttered as a wave of lust and hatred crashed through me.

"Mmm. You're so slick for me." His deep timbre was so utterly inhuman, which sunk straight between my legs, making me soaked and leaking enough arousal to dribble down my thighs onto the dirt. "You're the sweetest thing I've ever tasted."

His fingers slid through my folds, fat beads of arousal rolling down my thighs. I tried to clamp my legs shut, but he pushed them wider, and as he held me open by force, I realized I was only getting wetter. Shame radiated through me, making me burn hot.

I had no right to enjoy this. And I did. He knew it, too; he felt everything I did.

He knew just how drunk I was on this fucked-up dynamic we'd forged on that Easter night from Hell.

He pulled his fingers away from my center, placed his palm between my shoulder blades—his fingers still sticky with me—and pushed me down so my belly was flush with the ground. A few breaths later, warm beads of moisture peppered my backside, and I glanced over my shoulder.

The huge, furry beast was fully erect, the bright red glistening cock leaking copious amounts of pre-cum from the slit of his tapered tip. His hips canted forward so it dribbled onto my bare ass cheeks. When he caught me looking at him, he gripped his girth and gave it a few strokes.

"Give me one good reason why I shouldn't breed you right here in the dirt, Little Bunny."

There were a hundred reasons, and for some stupid one, I couldn't voice any of them. My mind said "no" while every other part of my body screamed "fuck yes."

The mere thought of him sinking into me, filling me with his cum, and the chance of his pack stumbling across us—seeing that he'd claimed the enemy for his mate—had me heating, fresh pheromones leaking from me.

And just like that, I was in heat all over again.

No. Oh gods, *no!*

This wasn't supposed to happen so soon, not after he'd fucked and marked me. And out here in the open, of all places.

My uterus clearly didn't give a shit. It cared about him and nothing else. The ultimate betrayal my body could've made.

Carver swore. "I said give me a good reason not to breed you. If I don't fill you up now, my pack might catch your scent, even with my mark."

A shiver shot through me, cold and warm at the same time. I could barely function with the pressure of my polarizing instincts trying to cleave me in half.

I wanted to kill him, even if it meant going down together.

I tried to scream, and immediately, his paw snaked around my throat, squeezing with enough force to leave me teetering on the edge of consciousness. "Don't you dare. They'll try to take you from me." His voice turned dark and deadly. "I'll spill pack blood if any of them so much as look at you."

The ability to breathe was beyond me, but now it had nothing to do with his hold on my throat. "Y–you don't get to pretend you care about me. I'm not b–buying any more of your lies. I know what you did to my sister."

CHAPTER

TWENTY-SIX

CARVER

Memories of the purple-haired girl from last year's round of sacrifices came rushing back. I'd never forget her, as she was the one Casey had caught. The one where I, for the first time, joined in on the feast.

Fuck.

The one time I tried to "fit" in with my pack and participate in the feast following the Hunt, it had to be Ruth's sister. Now I knew where I recognized that vibrant streak of purple running through her hair.

This was the moment where I was supposed to let my human side back into the driver's seat, the part of me that was better equipped to explain what had really happened.

Ruth scrambled to her feet and put several steps of distance between us.

"I didn't kill her," was all I could gnash out as I advanced on her, prowling toward my prey, ready to pounce if she tried to run again.

"You're a liar." Her voice shook as the space between us shrunk. Her survival instincts, along with our freshly forged

151

bond, made her all too aware of what her heat scent was doing to me. I couldn't resist the urge to fill and fuck her right here in the dirt for much longer.

Even if she was still under the impression that I'd murdered her sister.

"I'm not lying…" I said, taking another step toward her. "But even if I did, you butchered my brother. Would that not make us even?"

She held her ground, her hands fisted at her sides and the hatred in her eyes as sharp as daggers. "I— That's not— I didn't have a choice! You had a choice! You said yourself that you didn't need rabbit shifter blood to sate your blood-lust. Or was that a lie, too?"

"It wasn't."

I rose up on my hind haunches to reach for her. She stumbled backward, her back hitting a tree. "S–stay away from me."

"I can't." My mate smelled entirely too delicious for me to do anything of the kind. "My human should have known I wouldn't let you leave these woods without me."

Even though she hated me, her body was desperate for me. The delicious heat pheromones rolling up from her dripping cunt had my mouth watering and my dick hard.

Her attention dropped to my cock, and she sucked her bottom lip between her teeth at the way a thick rope of pre-cum oozed from the tip.

That look— It roused something savage inside me. Maybe I didn't crave bunny blood like the rest of my kind, but, oh, how I longed to wring every last drop of cum from her.

"Maybe he did know." I loomed over her now, one paw braced against the tree over her head.

She stiffened against the tree, fury licking up our bond

like fire on a rope. Her chest heaved, dark baby hairs clinging to her brow in perfect little curls. *She's so delicious.* Every moment I wasn't inside her was pure agony.

"Before, I thought this side of you—" she gestured to my furry chest "—was sweet and good. That you had this Jekyll and Hyde thing going on. But maybe there isn't that much of a distinction between you two. You're a monster in either form."

"I am," I agreed. "And that makes your pretty little pussy, oh so wet."

Contempt was written all over her face, but there was desire and excitement there too. Good. I wanted her to want me as much as I wanted her. I wanted her begging for my seed. If I caused her pain, it would be the kind that would leave her desperate for more.

And more than anything else, I wanted to take her far away from these woods, far away from her burrow and the people who threw her to the wolves.

"You're right. My human is a liar. Know why?"

My paw gripped her waist, giving her a squeeze. I loved how my claws nearly touched, she was so small in my grasp.

"Tell me." Her voice bent with a heady mix of pleasure and pain as my digits tightened around her.

The claw tipping my thumb brushed the underside of her breast, creating a lovely little indent in the soft mound. "He agreed to your arrangement, knowing full well I wouldn't allow you to leave. And he didn't tell you the truth when you assumed I couldn't breed you because he wants you just as much as I do. He accepts that now."

"You can't keep me here. They'll find and kill me."

"Oh, Little Bunny. I am leaving these woods with you. Even when I'm not there with you, you will always feel me.

I'll hunt those who mean to harm what's mine. I'll stalk your nightmares if it means being the only monster on your mind."

I canted my hips, pushing my cock against her. With our height difference, it jabbed at her belly, making her gasp. I simmered in her shock for a moment before drawing my hips back again, just to watch the thread of pre-cum attaching us stretch and snap.

She caught it, too. I knew by the way her pulse kicked up. She lifted her attention back to me, determination setting her jaw. "If you didn't kill my sister, then who did?" she demanded.

"My brother." I tilted my head, an ear flicking backward. "So, you got your revenge, don't you think?"

Her eyes slivered. "You still had a part in it, didn't you?"

"In a way," I admitted. "I wasn't involved in her death. I wasn't lying about that. I don't join in the Hunt. I never have."

She swallowed hard, giving me those fire-filled "fuck me" eyes.

The human locked within me warned me not to mate her out here in the open. But how could I resist her?

My mate was naked, the sweetest scent leaking from her cunt, so wet I could see little beads of her arousal streaking down her legs.

My mouth watered, my tongue snaking out to lick my jowls. Her lashes fluttered as beads of my saliva peppered her flushed cheeks. "Carver..."

My name in her mouth, breathy and threaded with lust, had me fisting my cock and pushing closer to her.

I needed to bend her over now. She was mine. All mine and I didn't give two fucks who or what might see us. Let them watch. Let them see as I knotted my mate.

"We can't. Not here."

"The cabin would be safer," I mused in my gravel cadence. "But you're in heat again. It won't be long before my pack scents it. It might be better to rut you here and cover you in my scent."

"What if they find us?"

"Then I'll kill them. I'll kill them all if it means protecting you."

Her beautiful doe-eyes widened with shock. "You'd kill your own pack? Why would you do that for me?"

The answer was simple, but I couldn't make myself voice it. I had no right to tell her I loved her, and she wouldn't believe me anyway. Besides, it's not like the love I had for her was healthy or normal. Oh no, my love for this little bunny was strange and dangerous, baptized in blood and hatred.

"I'll tear out every throat that stands in the way of your survival. I'll watch the whole world bleed for you, Ruthless."

TWENTY-SEVEN

gh. The mouth of this werewolf. With just a few dirty words and a look, my pussy was dripping. Something told me he'd be able to do that even when I wasn't in heat.

Fuck. Me.

I needed him. What was more, I *wanted* to need him.

When he said it was Casey who killed Sarah, I believed him. I could feel him telling the truth through our bond. I could feel almost everything. His guilt for what happened to my sister, even if he wasn't directly involved in her death. His concern for my safety, being out here in the open while his pack searched for me. The strongest emotion coming from the bond, however, was his hunger for me. It nearly drowned out everything else.

It was nearly impossible to hate him when I knew just how apologetic he was. All my fury dissolved like smoke, leaving this hollow sensation in my chest. He was right; I'd gotten my revenge, and I hadn't even known it.

I sure as shit hadn't enjoyed it. I felt robbed.

My mouth went dry, my body shaking. I needed to

distract myself, to fill this emptiness inside me... And what better way to do that than with Carver?

I reached out, my fingers curling around his massive cock. I loved how my fingers couldn't fully encircle his girth and how the texture of veins felt against my skin.

My gaze flicked up to meet his, and I sucked in a gasp at the way he regarded me, like a hungry animal ready to pounce on his prey.

I shivered, relishing that feral look in his eyes, knowing I was the one thing that stoked that fire inside him. I brought out the monster in him.

"If I take you right now, I won't stop myself from coming inside you. I will knot and breed you." His warning came out rough and guttural, sinking straight between my thighs.

I didn't know what he meant by "knot" but the word alone had my body burning with curiosity.

"Just fuck me already."

The pain, the pure need ravaging my body, was evident in my rasp. Fuck, I was practically begging him for it. And I would if he told me to. I'd do just about anything to abate the ache in my core.

"Run. Try to get away."

I couldn't stop myself from mirroring his wicked grin. I don't think I could ever get tired of this dark game of predator and prey.

I turned around and knew just how impatient he was to bury himself inside me, as he didn't let me get more than a few steps away before taking me down to the ground. I flailed helplessly, my nails clawing pathetically into the dirt.

The monster's brutal laugh sounded overhead, taunting at my faux attempts of escape.

Carver's shadow covered me first, and on the next pound of my heart, his muscular body draped over mine, dwarfing my tiny frame.

He rubbed his cock between my ass cheeks, the pre-cum leaking from his tip and allowing him to slide smoothly and easily over my flesh.

His hand pressed against the back of my head—gods, my skull was so small in his palm—and shoved my face into the dirt.

"Play dead, Little Bunny," he demanded with a soft growl that felt gentle and rough at the same time. His hot breath spilled over the back of my neck, and goosebumps prickled like sandpaper across my skin.

I twisted my head against the forest floor as best I could to peer up at him through his spread fingers. Had I heard him correctly? "Um, what?"

"You fucking heard me." His jowls curled back to reveal needle-sharp canines covered in copious amounts of saliva. "I caught my prey. Now, I feel like rutting it. I want to fuck your pretty little corpse. Play. Dead."

Every sinew in my body went tight, his dark demand making my skin crawl with horror and my pussy pulse and ache with mind-numbing need. Maybe I was right, the wall between wolf and man was blurring. They were growing closer as their personalities started to bleed together because this dirty little game could only come from the twisted mind of the man who'd told me to fuck the ax I'd killed his brother with yesterday.

Taking a breath, I steeled my nerves, shed the last remnants of my inhibitions, and went limp beneath him.

TWENTY-EIGHT

CARVER

I loved her like this, seeing her helpless, surrendering to me, even if it was all an act. Our dark little game that was all our own. When her body relaxed, I took her by the hips and lifted her ass in the air. My barreling breaths made the fine fur on her tail dance. It was cute watching her try to keep still for me.

With our size difference, I had to crouch over her, caging her against the earth as I lined our bodies up. Wicked amusement worked through me as I watched her struggle not to react to the fat cock slowly stretching her entrance.

Fuuuuck.

She was doing a fine enough job keeping still on the outside. Instead, her walls twitched and contracted around me, sucking me deeper inside. Her heart beat so hard that it tapped out a frantic rhythm against the head of my cock.

Sinking deeper inside her, the new position had my eyes rolling back into my head and my muzzle tipping to the sky.

A howl, as quiet as I could manage, bled from my

throat. It wasn't smart to make noise, but this woman had a way of bringing the animal out of me.

I fully seated myself inside her with a jab of my hips, and the slap of my balls against her clit had her whimpering.

I dropped to paint a lick over her cheek, chuckling lowly in her ear. "Dead bunnies don't moan when they're being fucked, Ruthless."

My hips picked up a steady pace as I fucked her hard and deep. The faintest trace of blood laced the air, and I guessed she was biting her lip hard enough to break the skin to keep herself from making a sound.

It's not that I particularly enjoyed her being quiet, but there was a sick part of me that enjoyed watching her struggle.

"Such a perfect, limp little bunny. Taking everything I have to give her," I growled against her nape, my jaws practically encircling her neck. My tongue slipped around her neck to feel the fresh mark on her throat.

My growl melted into a purr at the way her inner walls gripped me tighter as I tongued the scar. My hand moved to hold the base of her ears, pulling on them enough to lift her face from the dirt while my other arm banded around her stomach, pulling her back tight against my chest.

This position I had over her, the control... I knew it was only because she allowed it. This ruthless woman was small in stature, but fuck me, she was strong and brilliant. A survivor. A fighter. It was sexy as hell. Especially knowing her trust, this vulnerability wasn't simply a means to survival. It had turned into something more.

It was a gift. One I had every intention of possessing forever.

My rhythm didn't let up as I pounded her into the earth

without mercy, each thrust as savage as the last as I gave her what we both desperately needed.

Another moan slipped past her lips, strangled and lusty, sinking straight to my balls.

My hand found her belly, my fingers spreading over her supple skin. "I can't wait to see this belly swollen with my pup."

Her head jerked back to stick me with that bratty glare I'd come to crave. "D–dead bunnies can't get knocked up."

"Mmm. No, they can't." I nuzzled my muzzle into her hair and inhaled her intoxicating scent. "Imagining you healthy and happy... A knocked-up mate is a much better fantasy than you being my dead little bunny."

Ruth tossed her eyes as a phantom smirk shadowed the corner of her mouth where a string of drool trickled.

"And w–who said ro–romance was dead?" Her voice came out fractured, each syllable knocked from her lips with my every stroke.

My laugh came out dark and devilish. "Yes. I prefer you like this. Mouth running even as I rut you until you're drooling from both ends."

Her flesh beaded with sweat, making my fur cling to her, and my heart thundered in my chest, hammering a beat against her back.

When she groaned my name, I knew she was close. "You're mine, Ruth. Your mind. Your soul. Your heart. Your womb. It's all mine. Isn't that right?"

Black hair, with a flash of purple, lashed through the air with her frantic nod.

"Say it." I reached around, my possessive paw knitting into her pubic hair and giving it a gentle tug. "Who owns this pussy?"

"Y–you do." Her cry came out mangled as her release

wracked her body, making her spine arch against my chest. "Carver!"

"That's right, my ruthless little rabbit. Now, are you ready for my knot?"

Her head wobbled with a "Yes."

Another crazed grin stretched my muzzle. I doubted she knew what she was in for.

"I wonder how much of your alpha's seed your little cunt can hold?"

I didn't expect the coy smile she shot me, but it was that look coming with a thick moan that had me slamming into her in a series of quick, shallow thrusts, thick spurts of cum emptying inside her. Flipping her around in my arms while taking care to keep her speared on me, I positioned her to face me with her back against the forest soil.

I drew back far enough for Ruth to see the huge bulge at the base of my cock. Just as realization crept behind her chocolate orbs, I shoved my length, bulge and all, inside her.

"*Wha!* What's happening?"

"It's my knot, remember? It will keep us together while my seed seeps into you."

Pure, ball-obliterating pleasure whirled through me as her walls quivered around my cock, gripping me so tight, and I hadn't stopped coming yet.

Her eyes rolled into her head, and her fingers clenched the fur on my shoulders, holding on for dear life. "So much cum."

"All the better to breed you with, my dear."

She blinked at me, her brows gnashing at the reworked *Little Red Riding Hood* reference. "Wow. Original. Get that from your latest read, did you?"

I smiled down at her and settled on top of her in a way

that wouldn't crush her. We'd be locked like this for at least a little bit before the swelling would go down. "Oh, yes. The barbed wire face tattoo really howls Mother Goose."

She laughed, then sucked in a breath when my knot shifted inside her. "Fuck. H–how long do we have to stay like this?"

"Are you in pain?"

"No, it's just—" She released a shaky exhale. "Intense."

"Good. Just stay still for a little longer." I set to licking the dirt and sweat from her face, all the while emitting a low purr to keep her calm in my arms. Even the slightest shift would tug on her, and from the rutting I gave her, soreness had likely already set in.

I watched in utter fascination as she licked her lips, peering up at me through her dark lashes. "You're still hard."

"Of course I am. Look at you, naked and flushed. Your used pussy wrapped so tightly around me. If we were some-where safe, I could keep using you for hours."

At the mention of safety, her belly tightened beneath me. "What if they find us?"

"We were quiet enough, and now you smell of me. We should be fine."

Guilt wound tight around my chest, making it difficult to breathe. I shouldn't have mated her out here. The human side, the far more logical part of my being, didn't like that we were still out here. We needed to get moving as soon as possible.

"What do you want to do when we escape?"

She stared at me for a quiet beat, probably chewing on the "we" part. I tensed, preparing for her to argue. She'd forgiven me on some level, but that didn't mean she'd gotten comfy with the idea that we'd be leaving these woods together.

I could only hope she'd want us to be together as much as I did.

Pure relief washed through me when she smiled, a thoughtful look in her eyes. "Get a job that I actually get paid for. Preferably one that doesn't involve farming carrots. And go to concerts! Oh, go on a road trip! Or on a plane! Or–or—"

The endless possibilities had her lighting up, practically bobbing with excitement until she realized how we were connected and fell still again.

It was likely that Ruth hadn't traveled more than a few miles away from her burrow her entire life. The burrows were communes run like prisons when you compared how little freedom they were allowed. Our local one was especially restrictive. It was technically a democratic system they ran on where your vote mattered, but only so long as you were an Elder.

It occurred to me that our pack ran similarly. I hadn't done any of the things she was excitedly listing off, either. We were both victims, in a way. Born into cult life, with laws already in place meant to manipulate and exploit.

With our rutting, her heat state had ended, but fuck, she still smelled so damn good. She carried my scent now, my cum, my mark, the bruises from my grip and scratches from my claws covering her tender flesh in an obscene tapestry.

While I was inside her, the world melted away. Who we were and where we came from ceased to matter.

So, I didn't notice anything had approached us. Not until a familiar voice, wrapped in steel, called out to me from the trees. "Well, well. Look what we have here. Carver found himself a sacrifice."

My hackles bristled as a blond wolf stepped out from behind a tree. Lars rose up on his haunches, his flexing muscles making his fur ripple. "Looks like you've decided to have a little fun with your kill before avenging your twin. When do I get a turn?"

Fuck.

I'd been so stupid. So selfish.

These woods were big, but there had always been a chance they'd find us, and I'd fucked her out in the open anyway. That's what she did. She robbed me of all sense.

I remained crouched over her, raising off her body as much as the knot would allow. I could force it out, but there was a chance I'd hurt her. I could shift back to my human form, but then we'd be vulnerable.

Ruth gasped, and her pussy rioted around me. Alarm flooded her eyes as they pinged from tree to tree. "Carver. There's more."

One by one, my pack appeared. Some on two legs, some on four, approaching us from all directions. We were surrounded.

I wasn't a praying wolf, but I prayed then that Lila had done what she'd said and gone back to the pack house to rest.

Even from this distance, I could see Lars' wolfish sneer dip to where Ruth and I were still joined. His tail flicked behind him with his barking laughter. "Wait. You *knotted* her? You sick bastard."

Sparse laughter sounded as a handful of wolves half-heartedly joined in with the alpha.

"Does anyone else find this funny? Considering my father screwed a sacrifice, and Carver's father got his balls in a knot about it, then challenged him as pack leader. If I remember right, and I don't fucking forget, Carver, didn't you condemn my father too? Oh, the sweet irony. If only your father could see you now."

I ground my teeth together so roughly that pain shot through my gums. A warning growl rumbled from my chest. "Fuck off, all of you. This is my kill."

"You know pack tradition. You're expected to share."

"Not this time. She murdered my twin. She's mine alone to punish. When she's dead, I'll drag her back to the pack house. You vultures can have what's left of her."

For a moment, I thought Lars would take the bait.

His head tilted, his wolf ears flicking. His nose flexed as he breathed us in and took a step toward us, his line of sight going straight for Ruth's throat. "Is that— No. You didn't."

Lars' guarded demeanor turned hostile in a snap. He dropped back to all fours, his hackles raised, and his teeth bared. "He mated her. He mated Casey's killer!"

CHAPTER

TWENTY-NINE

RUTH

We were so totally fucked. Complete toast.

Stupid hormones drove us both to shag out in the open when there was an entire pack of wolves hunting me down.

I clung to Carver, trying to remain still and quiet on the off chance that he could talk his way out of this mess. A tall order considering his freakishly large werewolf dick was still hard inside me, the bulge keeping us locked in place.

Even the slightest jostle to our connection had his shaft sliding inside me, his cum making me ungratefully slick.

Whispers and growls of disapproval danced between the trees.

"He mated his meal?" one wolf muttered to another.

"No wonder he's never joined the Hunt. He thinks they're our equals."

"It's disgusting."

"A cat rutting a diseased rat would be more natural than this."

Carver's ice-cold eyes burned with malice. He radiated

violence and contempt. He didn't care about any of these monsters. Except for his brother's mate.

I scanned the tree line for the black she-wolf. She wasn't here, at least not from the little I could see while flat on my back.

The alpha slowly approached us. Carver growled, warning the male to keep his distance.

Lars stopped in his tracks. "Give me one reason why I shouldn't tear you to shreds and throw your bunny rabbit to the pack for dessert."

"I'll cut through half the pack before you take me down. Would you really throw all those lives away? Let's save the bloodshed. Let us go."

"Go? You'd abandon your unborn nephew?"

At that, Carver seemed to falter. A moment later, guilt leached into our bond. He didn't want to abandon Casey's mate, but he had every intention of doing that. For me.

For the rabbit shifter, he'd only met yesterday.

I still had bruises from when his human side tried to strangle me. Now, he was willing to betray his whole pack for me.

It was freaky how shit could flip so quickly. I felt like a different person than I did yesterday, and I knew he did, too.

When Carver didn't answer, Lars let loose another jackal-like laugh. "What a way to spit on your brother's memory, Carv. You know what? I'm feeling generous today. It is Easter, after all. I'll kill your mate first. Doesn't matter how addicted you are to her little cunt. No wolf can resist watching a rabbit be torn apart."

The alpha wolf prowled closer. The sinews in Carver's body pulled taut, he was coiled like a spring. Ready to lunge. If he did, RIP to my vagina.

"Come one step closer, and I'll tear out your goddamn throat, Lars."

"What, and wear your bunny rabbit as a codpiece?" The alpha raised his voice so every wolf that surrounded us could hear. "Looks like we're in for a show."

The alpha werewolf radiated arrogance, so of course, he took another step forward.

Everything that happened next moved at speeds my brain could barely keep up. Carver shifted. A werewolf in one blink and a tattooed, silver-haired man with death in his eyes on the next.

His knot disappeared with his wolf form and slipped out of me. He was on his feet, ready to shift again, but Lars was already lunging.

I hated feeling so helpless. If only I had the ax—

Before a plan had time to set in, a blur of black streaked across my vision. It slammed into the blond wolf hard enough to stagger him. The hulking alpha recovered in a beat, in just enough time for Carver to shift back into his wolf.

"Lila! Get back! The pup!" Carver hissed at the black she-wolf.

Lila lurched at Lars, ignoring the silver wolf's demands. The alpha snapped his attention as her jowls snapped at his legs. Jumping on yet another opportunity the black she-wolf opened, Carver lunged at Lars, pinning him to the ground.

I held my breath, expecting that the rest of the pack would jump to their alpha's aid. But the wolves only looked on as silent spectators, every last one of them frozen in place.

Sheesh. How much of a turd leader did you have to be for

no one to come to your aid when you're about to get your guts ripped to shit?

"Rip his throat out."

Lila hesitated at Carver's command. "You know the pack law. The wolf to kill the alpha takes his place. You have to make the final blow."

The silver wolf shook his head. "I'm not staying, Lila."

My throat throbbed with emotion. Even when he had an opportunity to lead his pack, he was still choosing me.

Lars struggled beneath Carver's hands, the downed alpha snarling and snapping at the wolf keeping him pinned.

Lila didn't hesitate another moment. She lunged, latching onto Lars' throat. The male wolf cried out when her teeth closed around his jugular, and with a twist and a sickening crack, he went limp.

The silence that stretched through the woods had my skin crawling. Not even the flora dared rustle as the wolves all stared their new leader down. If there was any hesitation about a pregnant, mateless she-wolf becoming alpha, no one dared say it out loud.

The wolves began muttering to themselves, nodding and chattering in agreement. Then, one by one, they all began to howl at the sky in broad daylight, sending birds exploding from the trees.

The woods came to life again, joining in on what was clearly some kind of pack ceremony.

Lila's bloody muzzle unlatched from Lars' tattered throat. Her attention flicked to me, her expression guarded and weary. I couldn't blame her. She'd watched me decapitate her mate.

"Is she really worth all this, Carv? Lars is dead. I— I don't know what to do as alpha."

I picked myself up from the ground, brushing off the dirt. I felt every eye turn on me.

Normally, I didn't mind being naked in front of other shifters. We couldn't take our clothes with us when we shifted, so in a way, we were part-time nudists. However, being naked in front of a pack of starving wolves was a different matter.

"You can start by renegotiating terms with the Elders of my burrow. It's the twenty-first fucking century. If it's rabbit shifter blood you need, we'll hire a mobile blood donation bus or some shit and deliver it to you in pretty plastic bags. I hear modern vampires do that. Get with the times, you fucking hicks."

"I can see why you like her," Lila mused, equal parts irritation and amusement underscoring her cadence. "She's ruthless."

Carver seemed to hold back a grin as Lila accidentally stumbled across the pet name he'd given me. "Casey would probably find this shit funny."

"Yeah. You both had twisted senses of humor." Stepping over Lars' body, the new alpha nuzzled Carver's chest. "I'll talk with the burrow. We'll be changing a lot of things around here. Go, Carver. Get out of here like you've always wanted."

"Will you be alright? The pup—"

"We'll be fine," she assured him with a hum. "You'll meet him one day."

IT TOOK Carver less than an hour to pack the possessions he wanted to take with us into the back of his old pickup. Most of the boxes were his books. I sat on the bench seat in the cab, wearing another one of his flannel shirts and, this time, a pair of his black briefs. It was all too big for me, but it sure beat driving to the next town naked.

"You look so fucking sexy in my clothes," Carver said as he stood beside the driver's side door, the last box in his arms. His gaze skated over my hair, and his grimace tugged at his facial tattoos. "What, no ears?"

"I can't be caught in my half-form when we drive into town. Don't worry." I tossed him a wink. "You can tug on them later."

He flashed me a filthy grin and disappeared, the truck sinking ever so slightly on its suspension at the extra box of books added to the truck bed. The door groaned open a second later, and Carver sat behind the wheel.

With his hand paused on the keys in the ignition, he eyed me for a moment, staring at me like he couldn't quite believe the turn of events over the last twenty-four hours. I never used to believe in fated mates, but what else could bring a bunny and a wolf together if not the universe and its twisted sense of humor?

Carver reached for me, tucking the purple section of my hair behind my ear before leaning over and planting a kiss on my temple.

When he chuckled against my skin, I angled my head to pop an inquisitive brow. "What's so funny?"

"It's just... Can you believe other people are opening Easter baskets, going to church, and doing egg hunts right now? And this is our Easter."

"That sounds so alien to me. People do that?"

He laughed again. "Oh, babe. You need to watch more TV. And that's coming from a book guy."

I giggled happily against his heat, then angled myself in my seat to examine the cardboard boxes through the cab's back window as he turned the ignition and started down the road. "No creepy animal heads?"

He laughed, raking a hand through his silver tresses. "I figured you wouldn't appreciate my hunting trophies. Wherever we end up settling, we can get new things. Things without any uncomfortable memories attached to them."

"Fresh start," I said with a small smile.

He started the truck, and as we drove away from the cabin, his eyes never went to the rearview mirror for so much as a glance at the old life he was leaving behind.

"Oh, by the way, I packed something for you." Keeping one hand on the wheel, Carver reached under the seat and pulled out the ax. Sometime in the last hour of packing, he'd found a moment to clean it.

He placed the ax in my lap. The weight of it felt familiar and uncomfortable at the same time. "I don't know," I hedged. "What happened to leaving uncomfortable memories behind?"

"It's complicated, sure. But that ax brought us together. Think where you'd be without it."

I opened my mouth to voice the rebuttal in my throat, but the words were swept away with my gasp.

There, on the side of the road, was a brindle bunny rabbit, running as fast as his small legs would take him.

Holy. Shit.

It was Sawyer.

Carver noticed him too on my next breath. "Is that—"

"Yeah. That's Sawyer, the male sacrifice I came in with."

At the corner of my vision, Carver's fingers flexed around the steering wheel, and a vein ticked in his jaw. "Are you going to tell me what he did to you now?" His voice was that dangerous and electric timbre from before.

"He..." I swallowed, my eyes darting back to the rabbit. "He took my first heat and the fact that he was around as an invitation to..." My voice trailed off. I didn't trust myself not to get emotional, and I was so tired of being angry.

Luckily, Carver didn't press the issue. And judging by the murder that flared behind his eyes, he got the picture.

"Wha—!" The truck took a sudden swerve off the dirt road, and my hands flung out to steady myself against the dash. The truck jolted, and I heard a sickening *thunk* as we ran over something.

Carver pressed the brakes, cut the engine and shot me a psychotic smile that had my body burning, his gaze centering on the ax balanced across my lap. "What do you say to us having one trophy head on the wall of our new place?"

My fingers curled around the wooden handle, and slowly, a smile as crazed as his own stretched my lips. "You got yourself another deal, wolf."

The End

About the Author

Aiden Pierce is a writer of dark paranormal romance and erotic horror. Her love stories are on the spooky side and usually end up with the monster or the villain getting the girl. She lives in the Pacific Northwest with her husband and their three fur babies.

You can find Aiden on any of these platforms:
Instagram @aidenpierceromance
Tiktok @aidenpierceromance
Her website www.authoraidenpierce.com

www.ingramcontent.com/pod-product-compliance
Lightning Source LLC
Chambersburg PA
CBHW071745150726

47998CB00005B/1808